"You're absolutely right," Jason said, and bent down and kissed her.

Then he promptly walked away, leaving Rosie to stare after him.

This time when he'd kissed her she hadn't jerked away. She'd been too tempted to throw her arms around his neck and give in to the kiss. His lips were solid and firm, and for the first time since leaving the Bar G ranch she felt warm inside.

But that couldn't happen, she reminded herself. And if Jason Barton was too much of a temptation she'd just have to get stronger...or avoid the man altogether.

There could never be anything between her and Jason.

Dear Reader,

Rosemary Wilson is a publicist in Cheyenne, but her heart is back on the family ranch in southwestern Wyoming. Then she discovers her father betrayed her by selling the ranch without telling her. Determined to keep the Bar G, owned by her mother's family for four generations, Rosemary approaches the future owner to try and convince him to tear up the contract.

Jason Barton is a multimillionaire who lives in Denver. He was raised on a small ranch and has decided to withdraw to a ranch close to the Rockies in Wyoming. But before he can buy the ranch of his dreams, he will give Rosemary one chance to reclaim her inheritance.

Rosie finds an unexpected ally she's not sure she trusts—and has a decision to make that will assure her of her dream...or not.

I believe in family, whether real family or family by choice. And I believe in fighting for what you believe. That's what Rosie and Jason are doing in this story.

I hope you enjoy their struggles and cheer them on.

Best,

Judy Christenberry

JUDY CHRISTENBERRY

Rancher and Protector

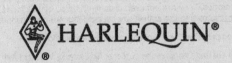

TORONTO • NEW YORK • LONDON
AMSTERDAM • PARIS • SYDNEY • HAMBURG
STOCKHOLM • ATHENS • TOKYO • MILAN • MADRID
PRAGUE • WARSAW • BUDAPEST • AUCKLAND

ISBN-13: 978-0-373-18277-0
ISBN-10:   0-373-18277-5

RANCHER AND PROTECTOR

First North American Publication 2007.

Judy Christenberry has been writing romances for fifteen years, because she loves happy endings as much as her readers do. A former French teacher, Judy now devotes herself to writing full-time. She hopes readers have as much fun reading her stories as she does writing them. She spends her spare time reading, watching her favorite sports teams and keeping track of her two daughters. Judy's a native Texan, but now lives in Arizona.

Recent titles by the same author:

HARLEQUIN ROMANCE
HER CHRISTMAS WEDDING WISH

SILHOUETTE ROMANCE
THE RANCHER TAKES A FAMILY

In the cowboy's arms...

They may seem tough on the outside,
but these courageous cowboys are honor-bound
and always true to their word.

As the sun sets over the raw beauty of this untamed
land and the stars light up the night sky, watch
sparks fly when our rugged ranchers meet their
match in a strong and loving woman.

If you love our gorgeous cowboys and
Western settings, this miniseries is for you!

The next WESTERN WEDDINGS story
is happening in May!

We're proud to present a debut novel by
Donna Alward

Hired by the Cowboy
is on sale in May
Only in Harlequin Romance®!

CHAPTER ONE

"I NEED to see Mr. Barton at once. It's urgent."

"I'm sorry, ma'am, but you need an appointment."

"But I've come from Wyoming and I need to go back this evening. Please, can you just get me a few minutes?"

"What is your business in reference to?"

"I'm here about the ranch he thinks he's buying."

That sentence got Jason Barton's attention. The door to his Denver architectural firm office stood open and he had heard the entire conversation between his secretary and the interloper. Normally he depended on Janice to deflect any unscheduled visitors, but in this case he hit the call button. "Janice, send the woman in."

He didn't *think* he was buying a ranch! He'd made a fifty thousand dollar down payment and was due to close the deal in two weeks. He watched the door, interested in seeing this person who thought differently.

A beautiful young woman appeared in the doorway, wearing a fashionable blue suit that displayed long legs and a trim figure. Her hair, auburn in color, was in some kind of fancy hairdo piled on her head. She exuded confidence as she entered his office.

"Mr. Barton?" Her voice was low, sexy.

He glared at her, refusing to be swayed by her appearance and tone. That had happened to him once before and the result had been devastating. "Yes?"

"I'm Rosemary Wilson. My father offered to sell our family ranch to you."

As if to dismiss her, Jason remained seated, not offering his hand. "Ms. Wilson, I suggest you talk to your father. I've made a down payment to buy the Bar G ranch and we're closing in two weeks."

To his surprise, her eyes filled with tears. What happened to the self-assured woman from a moment ago?

"I can't do that, Mr. Barton. My—my father died last week."

He frowned, studying her face as she tried to regain composure. "I'm sorry for your loss,

Ms. Wilson." He paused. Then he said, "But I'm afraid that doesn't cancel the contract."

The young woman lowered her eyes, no doubt struggling to regain her composure. Jason took the moment to appreciate her appearance, though he missed her big hazel eyes. He wouldn't be doing her bidding, but he wouldn't mind spending some time with her. Aside from the hour at the closing, of course.

Acting impulsively, which he rarely ever did, he said, "We could discuss the situation over dinner this evening."

She looked up at him and shook her head. "I have to get back to Wyoming this afternoon, but I could have lunch with you—if you're free."

Without responding to Ms. Wilson, he leaned forward and pressed the intercom. "Janice, get me a lunch reservation for two at the club."

"Yes, sir."

He looked up at his visitor. "If you'll let me sign a couple of papers, I'll join you out by Janice's desk in five minutes."

"All right."

He watched her walk out of his office and called himself every kind of fool. But he told himself he wasn't going to be taken in by another gold digger. He was just going to enjoy the company of a beautiful woman for a couple of hours. That was all this was.

And he certainly enjoyed entering the club with Ms. Rosemary Wilson on his arm a few minutes later. But once they were seated, she immediately began her plea.

"Mr. Barton, the ranch has been in my mother's family for four generations—"

He held up a hand. "I think we should order first, Ms. Wilson, don't you?"

She nodded, sitting back in her chair.

After the waiter took their orders and disappeared, Jason turned to her. "Now you can make your case."

"But it won't matter, will it?" she suddenly asked. "You have no intention of giving in to me."

"Probably not." He wouldn't lie to her.

"Then why am I here?" she demanded, and pushed her chair back to leave.

"Because I got the impression that your family ranch mattered to you, and I'd hear you out in case it mattered to me."

She stared at him and gradually relaxed in her seat again. "Very well. As I said, the ranch has been in my mother's family for four generations and I had no idea my father had intentions of selling it. Please reconsider, Mr. Barton."

He didn't want to reconsider. He'd fallen in love with the ranch in the foothills of the Rockies, away from city life. Having been raised on a ranch, he treasured the idea of returning to that life one day. He could understand the pride in the tilt of her chin at keeping the same home for generations. Too bad his father had sold his family spread. He stared into her hazel eyes, seeing the determination there at war with the fear of losing the homestead, and he could feel his resolve wavering. He wasn't so far gone that he didn't realize how unlike him this was. Normally he was steel-willed, a visionary with the strength and fortitude to back it up. But there was something about Rosemary Wilson…

He wouldn't give up his mission of owning a ranch. He'd find another place that he liked just as much as the Bar G. And Rosemary could have her family inheritance.

Still, he couldn't help feeling he wanted to keep the transaction quiet. If his business competitors discovered how he wavered on this deal, there was no telling what they'd try to get over on him.

With a sigh, he said, "All right, Ms. Wilson. I'll let you keep the ranch. Just return my down payment."

Having met her demand, he was surprised to see an uneasiness on her face.

"I—I can't."

"Can't what?"

"Return your money."

"You expect me to cancel the contract and take a fifty thousand dollar loss? I'm afraid I'm not in the business of losing money, Ms. Wilson."

"No, of course not. But if you'll give me one month, I believe I can return your money to you."

Before he could ask any questions, the waiter arrived with their lunch. He waited until the man walked away.

"How do you think you'll do that?"

"Apparently my father neglected a lot of things on the ranch, including roundups. My manager says there are a couple hundred head of cattle in the foothills. If we round up those cows and take them to market, I'd have enough to pay you back."

"That's all supposition, Ms. Wilson. I see no reason to give up the ranch based on such information."

"I understand that, Mr. Barton. But it's only a month, and I'm willing to make it worth your while."

He was interested.

"If I'm unable to make back the fifty grand," she said, "then I'll reduce the sale price of the ranch by an additional fifty."

"You realize you're risking a hundred thousand dollars? On the *possibility* you'll manage to raise fifty."

"I'm not an idiot, Mr. Barton. I know what I'm offering and keeping the family ranch is well worth the risk."

She folded her arms over her chest and glared at him.

"Eat your lunch and let me think," he ordered, not bothering to coat his words with sweetness.

She picked up her fork, but she didn't actually eat anything. He figured she was one of those women who ate a few lettuce leaves and claimed to be full.

His thoughts were interrupted when a woman stopped by the table to say hello. He recalled meeting the leggy redhead at one of the must-do business engagements he'd attended a few months ago. She effused and gushed all over him, batting her long lashes at him.

After several minutes, when he didn't ask her join them, she finally moved on.

Across from him Rosemary sat stiffly in her chair. "I'm sorry to be interrupting your social life, Mr. Barton."

Jason stared at her with jaded eyes. She didn't sound like she was sorry. And he wasn't sorry, either. He wanted nothing to do with any of the socialites in Denver.

"You weren't."

"I should've thought to ask your wife to join us," she said, no doubt trying to make him feel guilty.

"Not necessary. This is a business lunch." He didn't bother to tell her he had no wife now. He certainly didn't want her to think she could flirt her way out of the contract. Or, he suddenly thought, had she done that already?

He felt a little guilty taking advantage of her by agreeing to her deal. But she'd made the offer. He hadn't demanded it. He found it hard to believe that this woman could manage a roundup and recover cattle from the rough foothills of the Rockies. She didn't look like she could even stay on a horse, much less find the cattle.

Of course, she might try to fool him and sell cattle that had been counted in the contract. That thought had him changing his initial response. "I'll agree to your offer on one condition."

"What?" she asked, hope lighting her face.

"I and my ranch manager will accompany you on the roundup. After all, I need to make sure you don't try to sell cattle I've already paid for."

The anger on her face surprised him. "How dare you accuse me of trying to cheat you!" She glared at him. Then, after rethinking her lesser position, she changed her mind. "Fine. I don't care who comes. But if you try to sabotage our efforts or even try to slow us down, I promise I'll sue you for all you're worth." She jumped up and hurried toward the door of the restaurant, then she must have thought of something else, because she whirled around. "Be at the ranch for the start of the roundup at 6:30 a.m. Monday. And if you're late, too bad. We won't be waiting for you."

He gave her a small smile. "I wouldn't miss it."

* * *

When Rosemary reached the ranch that evening, she tried for an upbeat air, knowing Wes, her ranch manager, and Sara Beth, his wife and longtime housekeeper for her father, would be waiting.

And she should be upbeat, she told herself. After all, Barton had agreed to her proposal.

But the man was coming with them, she reminded herself. She didn't look forward to having Jason Barton on the cattle drive. He made her…uncomfortable, and she'd need all her wits about her on the roundup.

"What did he say?" Sara Beth asked as soon as Rosemary came through the door.

Wes was standing there staring at her. She tried to smile, but she wasn't very successful.

"He—he agreed to my proposal."

"So why aren't you happy?" Wes asked.

"He insisted that he and his ranch manager come with us."

"That's not an unreasonable request, Rosie."

"I know, but—but he makes me nervous. And he accused me of trying to cheat him!"

"That's only because he doesn't know you, honey," Sara Beth said, putting an arm around her. Sara Beth had been the closest thing to a mother for Rosemary since Linda Wilson had died ten years ago when Rosemary was fifteen. "He seemed real nice when he was here looking at the ranch. And he's so handsome!"

"I guess." Rosemary had no intention of raving about Jason Barton's appearance, even though the man was tall, broad-shouldered, with perfectly styled brown hair and the bluest eyes she'd ever seen. He was gorgeous, actually, and wealthy. But that didn't make him right. She was determined not to let his looks sway her, in spite of the unfamiliar feelings he aroused in her.

"So when did you tell him we'd start?" Wes asked.

"Three days from now. He's going to provide his own mounts and I told him not to be late. We're not waiting for him!"

"Now, Rosie, he's doing us a favor. Let's not make him an enemy." Wes turned to his wife. "Is dinner ready? I've got a lot of work to do for us to be ready by Monday."

"Yes. I'll just put it on the table. Are you ready to eat, Rosie?"

"Yes, I'll go change and then be back down." She ran upstairs, eager to put on comfortable clothes. Back in Cheyenne, she'd had to dress well as a publicist, but she no longer had that job. Now she was a ranch owner, she needed to feel the part. In her well-worn jeans and boots, she was able to think like a rancher. At least, that was what she believed, and now more than ever she had to give herself every advantage, real or imagined.

Over dinner, she and Wes discussed what they needed to do before the roundup began. Sara Beth added her opinion. She was not only an experienced cook, but she had occasionally gone on short cattle drives when she was younger.

Rosemary jotted lists, which was how she normally organized large projects at work. By the time Sara Beth finished the dishes, they had everything organized.

At least Rosemary hoped so. The roundup was too important. If she couldn't pull it off, she'd lose the only home she'd ever known. And she would know she'd failed her mother. Linda Wilson would've expected her to keep the ranch in the family. The Bar G was named after her mother's family, the Gables. They were long on hard work but short on sons to carry on the ranching tradition. That left it up to Rosemary.

As for her father, she wasn't sure she knew

what he would've wanted. After all, he'd sold the ranch.

She asked herself over and over why her father hadn't at least discussed such a big decision with her. She'd come home for the weekend only a couple of weeks before his fatal heart attack.

They'd spent some time together on horse-back and talked about her mother. It had been a special weekend. She'd remembered reiter-ating her promise to come home if he needed her. He'd looked a little tired, but she hadn't thought much about it, as ranching wasn't an easy life.

But it was a life she loved. She'd only gone to Cheyenne in the first place because her father had told her she needed to use her degree for at least a couple of years. She'd enjoyed her job and had learned a lot in Cheyenne. But her heart was here, on the ranch.

The memories of her mother and the times they'd shared had happened on the ranch. Her mother had taught her to cook, of course. But they'd also ridden together, though her mother had left the running of the Bar G to Robert, Rosie's father.

Then, after her mother's death, which had been devastating for a young teenager, she'd turned to her father, and had trailed after him all over the ranch. Though he'd always been disappointed that his only child was a daughter, not the son he'd wanted so desperately, he'd taught her all those things he would've taught a son. It hadn't been easy, but she'd learned them, along with rules he wouldn't have taught a son. Rule number one: Tears were forbidden.

But Robert Wilson wasn't here now, and she choked back those forbidden tears.

How could she survive without those memories? Without the ranch? She loved it here with the rolling hills, the mountain peaks in the distance. She loved being away from the city, where she could get up in the morning and look out her window and see blue skies all the way to the mountains.

So once again the question was why hadn't her father at least told her?

She'd discovered he'd used Jason Barton's down payment to pay off debts and set aside the rest to pay for his funeral. There wasn't much left. She hadn't wanted to give Jason Barton a discount on the price of the ranch, but she couldn't blame him for not giving her the month with nothing in return. She knew how powerful men like him operated. They always had to get something in return.

It was the stipulation he'd made that bothered her most of all. She didn't want to spend the two weeks of the roundup with the man. He was too handsome, too powerful, too…she didn't know what.

From her initial response to him, she knew it would take a lot of energy to resist that charming smile. Better to be angry with him than to let him get under her skin. She could lose her ranch and her heart if she wasn't careful.

Monday morning, Rosemary was up early. She had her breakfast at five-thirty and then gathered her bedroll and saddlebags, along with her father's rifle, and hurried out to mount up. She certainly wasn't going to be late.

But first she had to tell Sara Beth goodbye. "Thanks for all your work, Sara Beth." Just fifty years old, the woman was tall, attractive, with a slightly rounded figure. Her hair, blond with only a few strands of gray, rested in a mound atop her head.

"Child, you just be careful," Sara Beth replied. "And keep an eye on Wes. He still thinks he's a youngster, but he turned fifty-one last birthday."

"I know, Sara Beth. I'll make sure he doesn't overdo it."

"All right. Hurry home. I'm going to miss both of you."

Rosemary gave her a hug and then hurried out to the barn, where she could see Wes talking to a couple of men. They looked like cowboys, but Wes hadn't mentioned hiring anyone new.

When she reached the small group, she was shocked to see that one of the men was Jason Barton. He looked even better in well-worn jeans than he had in his designer suit and silk tie. Beside the barn was an expensive horse trailer attached to a dual-cab truck.

"Ms. Wilson," Jason Barton said in acknowledgment of her appearance.

She nodded in return. He wanted to keep it formal? That was fine with her. She looked to Wes to introduce her to the other man.

He did. "Rosie, this is Ted Houston, Jason's ranch manager. He's going with us, too, as you know."

She nodded again. "Fine. Are we ready?"

"Yeah, the boys have the horses ready. Your horse is tied to the corral, with the others."

"Is Cookie packed up and ready?"

"Yeah, he's already left. He's going to set up camp for us halfway there. We should make camp about four this afternoon."

"Good. Then let's mount up."

Without waiting for an answer, she turned toward the corral. Maggie, the sorrel mare she'd been riding since she was sixteen, stood waiting. Rosemary untied the reins, put her things on the saddle and then petted Maggie before she mounted.

Alongside Maggie was a gelding, large, strong, able to carry a big man like Jason Barton. A few days ago she'd faced him in spike heels, but today, in her cowboy boots, as was he, he towered over her.

As she swung into the saddle, he moved to the gray's side. Swinging into the saddle with great ease, he backed the horse up and moved in Wes's direction.

"Nice mount," she said quietly.

"Thanks. Shadow and I have been together for a few years."

"Did you bring a second mount?" All of

her employees had two mounts for the roundup because of the hard work.

"Yes, both Ted and I brought two mounts."

"Good. Take it from me, Mr. Barton. You'll need them."

Jason followed the woman up to the group of cowboys already assembled. He introduced himself to all of them, though he'd met some of them when he'd come to look at the ranch. He also introduced Ted.

But his gaze followed Ms. Wilson's movement. He'd been shocked by her appearance this morning. Gone was the makeup, the earrings, the designer suit and especially the spike heels. Even her hair was different. It was in a braid down the center of her back. Not only was she simply dressed, but none of her attire looked new. She acted as if this was a normal activity she'd been doing all her life.

He hadn't expected her to be experienced, but she sat her horse with ease. Maybe she knew what she was doing... Still, he wouldn't believe it until she proved herself on the roundup. Almost anyone could learn to ride a horse. Working on a roundup took more knowledge. Certainly Wes knew what to do.

He hadn't hired Wes to stay with the ranch because he felt the ranch was a little run down. He figured Wes was responsible for that.

Now Jason was beginning to wonder.

Wes set the pace at a lope. While Ms. Wilson stayed close to her manager, she seemed to know all the cowboys.

Jason had expected her to ride with the trail cook and to help with the meals. Not to round up the cows. Was her horse trained as a cutting horse? If the mare wasn't, its lovely rider wouldn't be of a lot of use on the drive.

Maybe she intended to supervise from camp, he suddenly thought. Only time would tell. Right now he was ready to do his best, to do the job in front of him. All his employees and business rivals would agree: Jason Barton believed in playing fair—as long as the other guy did, too. Guy or woman.

He clicked at his horse and Shadow obeyed, picking up the pace.

After about five hours Jason had to admit he was feeling stiff. A few weekend rides didn't equate to five straight hours in the saddle.

The irritating thing was that Rosemary Wilson looked as fresh as she had at 6:00 a.m.

Wes told everyone to dismount and eat their

bagged lunch under the shade of some tall trees. Like all the cowboys, Jason took care of his mount before he fed himself. There was a creek nearby and he led Shadow to it.

Rosemary Wilson didn't ask anyone else to take care of her mount. She led her horse to the water and waited until the horse had drunk her fill. Then she tied up the mare where the grass was green. Once her horse was grazing, she took her canteen and her sandwich and joined Wes.

Jason knew she wouldn't welcome him anywhere close to her; she'd communicated that clearly enough by her attitude. He joined them anyway, as did his manager, Ted.

"You certainly picked a nice day for the start, Ms. Wilson," Jason said, offering an easy smile to see if she'd relax a little.

She didn't. "Thank you."

"Do you think this kind of weather will last for the entire two weeks?"

"Who knows?"

"Wes, what do you think?"

"It's September. We sometimes get some cold fronts, even snow. But we're hoping, since it's at the beginning of the month, we'll be all right."

"How rough are the foothills we're going to be covering?" Ted asked.

Wes and Ms. Wilson exchanged a look. Then Wes said, "Some of it is pretty wild."

"We didn't bring rifles," Jason said. "Should we have?"

Wes looked him in the eye. "Yeah. But we've got rifles, so if we run up on a bear or something, we'll take care of it."

Jason turned to look at Ms. Wilson. "Did you bring a rifle?"

"Yes, of course."

"Can you shoot it?"

Wes laughed. "This little girl is one of the best sharpshooters I've ever seen."

The "little girl" only said, "Yes."

"I'm surprised, Ms. Wilson."

She raised one slim eyebrow. "Why?"

"When you came to my office, you looked like you had conquered the world of fashion, not sharpshooting."

"You were mistaken, Mr. Barton."

Wes frowned. "Are you two going to be so formal the entire roundup?"

"I don't mind Ms. Wilson using my first name, though I can't use hers unless she says it's okay."

"Come on, Rosie," Wes interjected. "Quit standing on ceremony. This is a roundup, not some fancy social affair."

Jason almost burst out laughing. He could see the stubbornness on her face. She wanted to remain cool, aloof, to hide behind formality. But she couldn't admit it in front of Wes.

Finally she acquiesced. "Fine. I'll be glad to call you Jason, and you can call me Rosemary."

"Thanks, Rosemary."

She nodded and took a bite of her sandwich.

Wes was watching him, as if he was wondering why Jason was pushing Rosemary from her comfort zone. But as Wes had said, they couldn't be formal for two weeks.

In spite of Wes's bragging about Rosemary's skills, Jason still wasn't sure she would be of much use on the cattle drive. He would just have to wait and see.

After a half-hour break, they were all in the saddle again, facing another four to five hours before they reached their first camp. Wes had explained that they would be at the halfway point this evening. Then they would travel another eight hours the next day. The day after, they would begin the search for cattle, at the farthest point and the highest elevation, beyond which the terrain was too rough for cattle to venture. Then they would gradually move back toward the ranch, sweeping the hills for the cattle.

It would be a much slower trip coming back than it had been going.

When they reached the camp set up by the cook, they could smell dinner cooking and see a large campfire. The warmth would be welcome, Jason admitted. As the sun lowered behind the hills, the air had changed from crisp to cold.

And the food would be just as welcome. His body was tired and in need of fuel. He'd tried not to slump in the saddle because Rosemary certainly wasn't slumping. The woman must have a lot of muscles in that trim figure, he reasoned.

Ted was apparently feeling much as he did. "I'm glad to see that fire. I don't like the cold."

Jason frowned in surprise. "Haven't you had to go out in bad weather to take care of the cattle?"

"I usually get some of the men to do that work."

Jason thought he knew Ted Houston fairly

well. He'd come highly recommended, and he'd ridden with Jason on a couple of weekends at a stable outside Denver, where Jason kept Shadow and several other horses. But a leader didn't ask his men to do things he wouldn't do.

After they dismounted and tended their horses, including putting up a rope corral that would hold the horses for the night, they all moved quickly to the fire where the cook had an appetizing stew cooking over the fire.

"It smells good, Cookie," Rosemary said, finally smiling.

"It's Sara Beth's recipe, Rosie, so you know it's good." He turned to Jason and held out a hand. "I don't believe I've met you. I'm Albert Downey, but everyone calls me Cookie, for obvious reasons," he said with a grin.

Jason shook his hand. "Glad to meet you. I'm Jason Barton and this is Ted Houston."

"Welcome, boys. The tin bowls are stacked on the tailgate of the SUV. Grab one and a spoon and get in line. It's chow time."

Jason waited for Rosemary to advance first. He fell in step behind her, his eyes on the sway of her hips in those tight jeans. They'd ridden through some of the most beautiful scenery in the west today, but Jason had to admit this was the prettiest sight he'd seen all day.

CHAPTER TWO

As HE walked to the SUV, Ted came up alongside Jason. "That Cookie obviously doesn't
know who we are," he said with an edge to his
voice. "If he did, he'd be more respectful."

Jason spared him a quick glance. "We're
helping with the roundup, Ted, nothing more.
There's nothing wrong with how he treated
us." He took a bowl and spoon and moved
after Rosemary who had gone to get her bowl
and spoon in front of him.

But she wasn't the first one in line. Others
had gone before her. She wasn't standing on
ceremony as Ted seemed to expect. Jason had
to admit he was fascinated by Rosemary, but
he assured himself it was only because of the
contrast between the woman as he'd seen her
in Denver and the woman who stood before
him now.

When his bowl was full, Jason followed

Rosemary to the canvas stools Cookie had set up around the fire. Selecting the one next to her, he sank down, relieved to have canvas under him instead of leather.

"Long day?" Rosemary asked.

"Yeah, but you seemed to hold up well."

"I've done this before."

"Surely not recently."

"No, not recently. My father let things slip on the ranch the last two years."

"I thought maybe it was Wes's fault." Jason didn't mean his remark as an insult, but he realized he'd offended Rosemary again.

"How dare you?" she said before she stood and moved to another camp stool, making her disdain obvious to everyone gathered around the fire.

Wes, who was just now being served as the last man in line, watched Rosemary as she moved to another seat. Then he crossed to the seat she'd abandoned and sat down.

"How you doing, Jason?" he asked.

"Fine. Cookie makes a mean stew."

"Yeah, he does."

"Who is Sara Beth? He said it was her recipe."

"She's my wife. She's been the housekeeper

on the ranch for a long time. That's how I met her."

Conversation had resumed around the fire. The men had all been watching Rosemary, as if to determine she was all right. But with Wes's approach and general conversation, he'd apparently reassured his men.

"What did you say to Rosie?" Wes asked, his voice lower.

"I'm sorry, Wes. I spoke without thinking. She thinks I insulted you."

"How'd you do that?"

"She said her dad hadn't done much on the ranch the last two years. I said I'd thought it was your fault."

"That's not unreasonable." Wes took a spoonful of the meat and vegetables. "Rosie is a little touchy about things right now. She feels she abandoned her dad when he needed her. In truth, the old man sent her away. I think he was just too tired, and didn't want to admit that to her."

"That must've made things hard for you."

"Yeah, but I couldn't abandon him or the men who worked for him. And Sara Beth would never have agreed to leave him or Rosie."

"I see," Jason said. "I'm sorry I upset her. I didn't realize the circumstances. I'll apologize to her whenever she'll let me."

"No need. I'll talk to her. Just remember this is a hard time for her. Give her a little space."

Jason knew what Wes was telling him, but something inside him didn't want to listen. "I'll be more careful about what I say to her."

Wes gave him a considering look, and Jason tried to conceal his response. He didn't want Wes to forbid him to talk to Rosemary.

"Okay. I'll try to patch things up when I talk to her."

Jason let out a soft sigh. "Thanks, Wes. I appreciate it."

"No problem. We don't want any fights in front of the men."

"No, of course not."

Rosemary watched Jason and Wes out of the corner of her eye as she ate her stew. She would demand Jason leave if he upset Wes. She wasn't going to allow that. Wes and Sara Beth were her family—her only family, now that her dad was gone.

Her eyes filled with tears at the thought of

her father. He'd obviously been too tired, too ill, to handle the running of the ranch. Wes had apologized to her, but he'd said her father wouldn't agree to anything that required any money. Clearly he'd been in financial difficulty, too, though she hadn't known. She wondered if Wes and Sara Beth had even been paid all their wages, though they'd both told her they had.

The biggest question, for her, had been whether Robert had sold the ranch because he didn't believe she, a female, could handle running it. Even thinking the thought that she'd hidden in her heart almost brought her to tears.

One of the cowboys sitting next to her leaned over and said, "You okay, Rosie?" Apparently mistaking her upset, he added, "If the man got fresh, we'll take care of him."

"No! No, I'm just tired, Nick. There's no problem." She even managed to smile. "I'm just thinking about my dad. I wish he was here."

"Yeah, he was a good man. We all miss him."

"Thanks," she said softly and finished her stew. She certainly didn't want the men to think Jason Barton had insulted her. In truth, he'd insulted Wes, but she supposed she couldn't hold it against him. He couldn't know why things had gone downhill at the ranch.

After she finished her meal, she carried the bowl over to the big tin dishpan Cookie had filled with hot, sudsy water. Each man was expected to wash his bowl and spoon and put them back on the tailgate of the SUV. She had suggested that system when, as a teenager, she'd come out on a roundup and seen how hard Cookie had to work.

Rosemary was glad Jason followed Wes to the dishpan to wash his own bowl. Then he motioned to Ted to do the same. She noticed Ted's reluctance until Jason spoke to him. From what she'd seen of Ted in one day, he seemed ill equipped to lead men. Especially the men on her ranch who were accustomed to a fair, hardworking manager like Wes.

What would happen to Wes and Sara Beth? Surely they would lose their jobs if Jason got the Bar G. Would they hook up with another ranch in the area? She didn't want to lose touch with the couple she loved dearly. Another reason to fight for her ranch.

She retrieved her bedroll and saddle where she'd left them near the rope corral. She'd put her bedroll next to Wes, and he'd keep an eye out to be sure she was undisturbed by anyone.

Not that she'd expect any of the men who worked for them to be a problem. Everyone had worked there for years, except for Nick, and he'd never caused a problem in the time he'd worked for them.

But with Jason and Ted in the mix now, she wouldn't take any chances.

Wes got his bedroll and saddle and joined her. He always had her put her bedroll next to the SUV and he slept on the other side of her. They followed the same routine tonight.

"You okay, Rosie?" Wes whispered.

"Yes. I'm sorry about that. I know it was rude."

"What he said was reasonable, you know. He didn't know any of us."

"I know, Wes, but it upset me that he'd criticize you for Dad's behavior."

"Don't worry about it. He understands now. So everything's okay?"

"Yes, of course."

"All right. Go take care of business while I keep an eye on everyone."

When she returned a few minutes later, she found Wes talking to Jason again.

She spread open her bedroll and sat down on it to remove her boots. Then she tucked them in the bottom of her bedroll.

"Why are you doing that?" Jason asked, distracted by her movement.

"Doing what?"

"Putting your boots in the sleeping bag."

"Because I don't want any creepy crawlies in there when I put them on in the morning."

Jason raised his eyebrows and looked at Wes. "Does that happen?"

Wes chuckled. "Not often. But it happened to Rosie once, and she refuses to leave her boots out of her bag. But she's got a little more room in her bag than most of us, 'cause she's a lot shorter."

Rosemary ignored the two men and settled her head on her saddle after removing her coat and pulling up the sleeping bag.

Jason was staring at her, but she pretended not to notice.

"If you're worried, you can set your boots inside the SUV. Cookie doesn't mind," Wes told him.

"Nope. I'm not asking for special treatment. Where shall I bed down?"

"Anywhere near the fire. But be sure you

leave Cookie a pathway. He'll be putting wood on the fire in the morning so he can cook breakfast."

"How about I put my roll next to you?" Jason asked.

"Sounds good to me," Wes said with a grin.

Rosemary ground her teeth. At least Wes was beside her. She'd never sleep a wink if she thought the sexy millionaire was in the next bedroll. Her nerve endings seemed to be on full alert whenever Jason was near.

Slowly the camp settled down. The only noise was the crackling of the fire, even though it was banked up so it wouldn't spread, and the howling of the coyotes and wolves.

Cookie's activities the next morning awakened Rosemary. She unzipped her bedroll and immediately shrugged into her coat to ward off the cold. The sky in the east was showing some light, but the sun hadn't yet put in an appearance.

Taking her boots out of the bedroll, Rosemary pulled them on just as Wes sat up. She silently motioned to tell him she was going away from the SUV for a few minutes. His nod meant he'd make sure none of the men went in that direction. When she reappeared, Jason was awake, too, though most everyone else was still asleep.

Cookie had the big coffeepot on the fire and he was getting out the huge skillet he used every morning. Without saying anything, Rosemary got out a large bowl and began breaking eggs in it.

She saw Jason lean over and whisper something to Wes. Though she wondered what he was asking, she forced herself to ignore him. Wes would take care of whatever was his concern. The scent of coffee was waking up the men as much as the small noises Cookie and Rosemary were making. In another five minutes, everyone would be up.

Wes led Jason to the stack of tin coffee cups. After each taking one, they made their way to the fire and Wes poured them both a cup of coffee. They squatted down by the fire, cowboy style, and enjoyed their drinks.

Rosemary handed Cookie the bowl of beaten eggs and took out a loaf of bread he had baked in advance. Taking a sharp knife, she put the bread on a cup towel and began slicing it into fifteen slices, one for each person on the roundup.

"Grub's ready," Cookie called.

The men hurried to get their tin plates and get in line for breakfast. Rosemary set the bread in a tin plate near the fire. Cookie served up the bacon and the scrambled eggs.

When Ted received his eggs and bacon, he reached for two pieces of bread. Without hesitation, Rosemary said, "Ted, we each get only one piece of bread."

"But there's extra."

"Because Wes, Cookie and I haven't eaten yet."

Behind her a quiet voice said, "Ted."

That was all Jason said, but Rosemary figured Ted could hear the threat in it as well as she could, because he returned the top piece back to the plate. "Sorry," he muttered and walked away.

Nothing else was said. They seldom had conversation in the mornings. Some people didn't want to chat while they were still waking up.

As everyone got ready to ride out, Wes called out, "Has everyone filled his canteen?"

Several nodded since they'd done this for years, but there were always a couple who forgot. Jason and Ted came back to fill theirs, too.

Rosie was looking forward to the start but

she couldn't help worrying about riding with Jason. She felt her life would be simpler if he left. He just made her nervous. And that was unusual for her. In Cheyenne, she'd never felt nervous whether she was speaking to the press or making a presentation to a client. Of course, her "clients" were other states. She worked for the State of Wyoming, promoting tourism. It had been a dream job.

Wes rode up, leading her second horse, a dun named Sandy. He always saddled her horse while she helped Cookie. "Here you go, Rosie. Maggie looks good today, but I thought you should give her the day off."

"Of course. Yesterday was a long haul. Today won't be quite as long, will it?"

"Not in distance, but the ride will be rougher as we move on up into the foothills."

"Will Cookie be able to drive as far as we need to go?"

"Almost. We'll head farther north before we turn back toward the ranch. He won't have to move far for the next camp."

"Good. He'll need a little rest after yesterday and today."

"I know." He waited until Rosemary was in the saddle and got her sandwich before he headed out. The rest of the party was waiting for them.

"Watch for rocks so you don't lame your horse," Wes called out to the cowboys. "We'll be riding a little slower today because of the roughness of the terrain." Then he led them away from camp.

About half an hour later, Cookie passed them by in the truck, waving a hand as he continued on to the ultimate camp.

Rosie glanced over the cowboys, at the two men in the rear who led the extra mounts on two long ropes. When she caught Jason's eye, she quickly looked forward. If she looked at him very often, he might realize how fascinated she was with him. Besides, she didn't want to be the one who caused her horse to go lame because she wasn't watching.

To her surprise, Jason rode up beside her.

"Everything all right?" he asked.

"Yes, of course. Everything all right with you?"

"Sure."

"Was your wife upset about you being away for several weeks?"

"No."

"I'm glad she—"

"I don't have a wife," Jason said abruptly.

Rosemary stared at him. When she'd learned he was the supposed buyer for the ranch, she'd look him up on the Internet. In addition to his successful architectural business she found pictures of Jason and his beautiful wife attending society events in Denver. "But I saw—"

"We're divorced."

"Oh. Sorry." She spurred her horse to move a little faster, but Jason fell back beside Ted. Just as well, she told herself, now that she knew Jason Barton was a bachelor.

When they reached camp that afternoon, the sun was just sinking over the rims of the Rockies. In a matter of minutes, it was dark, in spite of the millions of stars visible at night. Rosemary loved the sky out on the ranch. In Cheyenne, there were a few too many city lights.

Cookie had everything ready to eat as soon as they'd taken care of the horses and put up the rope corral. They'd picked their way through the rocks and foothills and the ride actually took longer than the ride yesterday. No question but that everyone was hungry.

Tonight, Cookie had made skillet meat loaf and a pot of vegetables. After he'd served everyone, he promised mashed potatoes tomorrow night since he wouldn't be traveling a long distance.

Of even more interest was the chocolate cake he set on the tailgate of the SUV. "Now don't you be thinking I made this cake. Sara Beth sent it along. I just had the feeling you'd appreciate it more tonight than you would've last night," Cookie informed them all.

There was a cheer from around the campfire and Cookie grinned at them. "I'll tell Sara Beth you're much obliged." Then he filled his plate and sat down to eat.

Rosemary kept an eye on Ted. She couldn't help thinking he might do something wrong again. After he'd eaten his dinner he started to get up, but Jason, who was sitting next to him, said something and Ted sat back down.

Jason must've figured out that no one got dessert until Cookie finished eating. A cook on a roundup worked hard, and he needed to have time to eat his meal. Rosemary wondered what kind of a roundup Ted ran, or if he ever had.

Maybe she'd ask Jason that question if she got a chance.

When Cookie finished his meal, he cut the cake and served each cowboy his piece in his own plate. Even Ted accepted his cake with good spirits.

Jason, who was sitting next to Wes, leaned over and asked something, but Wes smiled. Rosemary wondered what Jason had said that amused her manager. She'd have to remember to ask Wes later.

She guessed Jason had convinced Ted to follow the rules. He certainly hadn't caused any problems this evening. He was even making conversation with the cowboys around him.

Rosemary let out a breath she hadn't even realized she was holding. But when Jason squatted down beside her, she jumped.

"Is everything going okay?" he asked with that charming smile that always made her pulse accelerate. She told herself she was safer if she kept her eyes on her cake, rather than the man too close to her.

"Yes, of course, everything's going well. Doesn't Wes think so?"

"I assume so. He hasn't said anything to me about any problems."

Which made Rosie think of his prospective manager. "Have you ever seen Ted in action, on a cattle drive?"

"No. But he came highly recommended. You can be sure I'll be looking at that recommendation again when I get back to Denver."

"I'm not trying to pressure you, but Wes and Sara Beth will be out of a job if you get the ranch. I would feel better if you hired them in place of Ted."

"I've been wondering if you would mind me hiring them."

At that, she turned and looked at him, and was struck by his deep blue eyes dancing in the firelight. Her effusive enthusiasm tempered into a more professional tone when she finally was able to speak. "I'd be pleased." She cleared her throat. "If you get the ranch, I'll go back to Cheyenne, but I'd keep in touch with them. I want them to be happy, and I can guarantee their work."

"What exactly did you do in Cheyenne?"

She was surprised by that personal question—and more surprised that she answered. But Jason seemed to be drawing her in, and like an oppositely charged magnet she had no choice but to go. "I worked in publicity for the Tourism Department of the state government."

"You mean you're responsible for those catchy ads about visiting Wyoming?"

"Well, I worked on the team that came up with them. They were great, weren't they?"

"Yes, they were. I'd looked for some land in Colorado, but after seeing one of those ads, I turned my attention to Wyoming. I wanted somewhere with roads less traveled," he said, almost quoting the ad.

She smiled. "I'm glad you liked it, and I suppose I'm glad you considered Wyoming." She shook her head. "Will you look around Wyoming again if I get to keep the ranch?"

"Probably." He gave her a devilish grin that nearly stopped her heart. "Shall I hire Wes and Sara Beth even if I don't get the ranch?"

She wagged her finger in front of him. "Oh, no. They'll stay with me. But if you do get the ranch, I'd like you to consider them. They're the best."

In a quick action he snagged her finger, their first contact sending shivers up her spine. "And what do I get if your guarantee doesn't pan out?" he asked in a low voice.

"You can name any penalty you want, because I'm sure of my guarantee."

"Fine." Then he leaned in close to whisper in her ear, "If I'm not totally satisfied with their performance, you owe me a kiss."

She almost fell over as she jerked away from him. Jason Barton was a smooth operator—and she'd best remember that. And their deal. She lifted her chin in an indignant pose. "Don't hold your breath!"

CHAPTER THREE

THE NEXT morning as they all sat around the campfire eating breakfast, Wes organized them. They would begin their search in groups of three. Of course, since Cookie wouldn't be rounding up cattle, Wes ordered two men to help Cookie move the spare horses and set up the rope corral in his new camp. Then they would maintain the cattle the others brought back to the camp. That left four groups of three.

To Rosemary's surprise, she was in with Wes and Jason. Since Jason showed nothing on his face, Rosemary wondered if he'd talked to Wes earlier. They had again gotten up a little early and drunk their coffee by the fire.

"After you finish breakfast and wash your dishes, let's mount up." Wes had given each group an area to search, so they wouldn't overlap each other.

Rosemary helped Cookie pack, as she usually did, and Wes saddled her horse for her. Today she'd be riding Maggie, which eased any tension she might feel. Maggie had been trained by Wes, and she was a great horse.

Wes, mounted on his horse, led Maggie over to the SUV. "Here's Maggie, Rosie. You ready to go?"

"Sure. Where's Jason?" Not that she really cared, she told herself. But he was a part of their team.

"He's coming."

As Rosemary swung into the saddle, Jason joined them. "Are we taking a lunch with us today?"

"Nope. Cookie will have something ready later, after he moves the camp. If we get hungry we can grab something when we bring in any cattle we find," Wes explained. "Did you talk to Ted?"

"Yeah. I'm not sure he'll be of much help. I'm beginning to think he's a complete fraud."

"Could be. He doesn't seem to understand how to blend in with the other cowboys," Wes said as he led them toward the area they were to search. "You, on the other hand, seem a natural."

Jason chuckled. "I'm just following your lead, Wes. You're the expert." Then he added, "You and Rosemary. If you'd told me last week that she'd blend in anywhere, I wouldn't have believed you."

"I don't see why not!" Rosemary said, irritated.

Both Wes and Jason laughed.

"What's so funny?"

"Have you ever looked in a mirror?" Jason asked, turning in the saddle to stare at her.

She frowned. "Of course I have. What are you talking about?"

"You're a beautiful woman, the only woman, in a band of cowboys. But they treat you like you're one of the guys. It's amazing."

She ignored the compliment. "I've known most of them for years, and they know Wes would fire them on the spot if they harassed me. So I don't think it's so surprising."

"I guess you're right." He faced forward again and tugged on his hat. After a few seconds he asked, "So you always accompanied your father on the roundups?"

"No. I wanted to, but Mom wouldn't let me. After she died, though, Dad always brought me along." She remembered the times she'd spent with her father on horseback; they were her best memories. Out on the roundups they were equals, each with a job to do, each relying on the other. Memories—good memories—flooded her, and emotion built in her throat.

"He didn't have a son, and he talked about how I'd need to understand ranching if I was going to run the place after he was gone." Overwhelmed, she ducked her head as tears began to well in her eyes.

"Rosemary, I'm sure he—"

But she never got to hear his remark because Wes called out, drawing their attention.

"We've found the first of the cows. Let's circle behind them."

There were about fifteen head grazing, appearing undisturbed by their approach. Wes silently indicated where both Rosemary and Jason should go. Then they began driving the small herd toward the new campsite.

Rosemary eased up on a steer that had come to a halt. She had her lariat out to use to prod the reluctant animal. She slapped the steer on its rump. To her dismay, the steer turned and charged her.

Even as Maggie jerked out of the way,

Rosemary heard both Wes and Jason yell. But Rosemary reined her in, struggling to stay in the saddle.

"Rosie, are you okay?" Wes asked as he raced to her side.

"Yes, I'm okay. Maggie took care of me."

"He turned on you so fast, neither Wes nor I could get here in time," Jason said. "Do you need to get off your horse and rest?"

"Not with that killer steer in the neighborhood. I'll let you two deal with him," she said with a shaky laugh.

"Right," Jason agreed and turned his mount to force the steer back into the herd.

"I think Jason's got his number. Are you okay to go on?"

"Of course I am, Wes. Thanks to Maggie."

"Okay. I'm going to let you and Jason take this little herd on in and I'm going to search out more cows. I'll see you two in a little while.

"I don't think you should, Wes. It's not safe to be out here alone."

"I know Sara Beth made you promise to take care of me. That's ridiculous, Rosie. I'm a grown man and I've been doing this kind of work all my life. But I'll be careful, I promise. And you do the same."

"Okay," Rosemary agreed, but she wasn't happy about it.

"Keep an eye on her, Jason," Wes said.

Rosemary huffed in indignation. "I've been doing this all my life, too!"

Jason grinned. "Come on, Rosie, we've got to get moving so we can get back quickly."

She was so used to Wes calling her Rosie that she didn't even realize Jason was using her nickname until it was too late to protest. She'd have to do that later. Right now the cows demanded her attention.

It only took them about half an hour to reach the new camp. The two cowboys left to maintain the herd were having a cup of coffee with Cookie. When they caught sight of Rosemary and Jason's herd, they mounted their horses and met them.

"Good job! Where's Wes?" asked Nick, the newest hand.

"He's looking for more cows," Rosemary replied. "We've got to get back with him. Have you got these?"

"You bet! Be careful," Nick called as she and Jason turned back to retrace their trail.

"I think that cowboy has a crush on you," Jason said as they rode along.

"Who?" Rosemary asked.

"Nick. He watches you all the time."

"I'm sure he doesn't," Rosemary protested.

"I know he does. I've watched him."

"He's probably thinking the same about you."

"What? That I've got a crush on him?"

She laughed, in spite of herself. "Why are you watching him?"

"Because he's watching you." After a moment, he added, "Wes and I talked about it. He said he thinks the same thing. He's keeping an eye on things."

"He always keeps an eye on everything. Wes is a great ranch manager."

"I know he is. You don't have to sell me on him. I've already talked to him about staying on if I get the ranch."

"Did he agree?" Rosemary asked anxiously. She hoped he would. She knew Wes and Sara Beth would be happy staying there with Jason. He would be a good ranch owner.

The admission surprised her. But it was true, she realized. In just these two days Jason had exhibited some of the most important qualities for an owner, including his willingness to perform any task he'd asked of his men.

Still, Rosie wondered how he'd own the Wyoming ranch when his business was in Denver. She asked him.

"I was wondering when you'd be getting around to asking me that," he said. He reined his horse out of a gallop to answer her. "I intend to live here full-time."

"So you'll be closing your architectural firm, then?" From the looks of the plush offices, she figured it was successful.

"No, I'm not retiring yet," he said with a laugh. "Actually, it's a long story. You see I'm an architect by trade. But during the summers to earn money for college, I worked for a builder. After I got my degree, I designed some apartment buildings. I had to finance the first one myself. I intended to sell it once it was built, but I ended up keeping it. And I've gone on from there. I now have six apartment buildings in Denver that I own, plus I design other things, like malls and office complexes."

"Do you own them, too?"

"Only some of them."

So Mr. Barton was even richer than she'd thought. Would he ever be satisfied with the simple life of a rancher? Out here there wasn't much call for a tuxedo and shiny shoes. Surely he'd figured that out. Deciding she had to ask, if only to protect Wes and Sara Beth, she said, "Are you sure you're going to fit in out here?"

Jason grinned. "Absolutely. I can't wait to leave Denver. I can do all my work from the ranch. I'll fax my designs to my clients. I'll have to go to the city to check on the progress of the construction and, occasionally, on my apartment buildings, but other than that, I'll be a rancher."

Somehow she could picture him in that role all too easily. "If you're into architecture, why do you ride like you were born to it?"

"I was raised on a small ranch outside of Denver. We had a couple of horses and I started riding as a little boy."

"Why not go back there?"

"Because the city has overtaken the property. My parents sold it ten years ago for a nice sum and moved to Arizona."

"Quite a change. Seems—"

Just then Wes called out their names. She looked up ahead for Wes, but she didn't see him.

"Where is he?"

Jason pointed up on one of the slopes above

them. "Up there. Looks like he's found more cattle." Jason picked up his speed and Rosemary followed.

When they got close to Wes, they pulled up and looked at him for guidance. He'd found almost another twenty head of cattle, but they were spread out on rocky terrain. For a moment, the only sound was the wind blowing through the aspen trees.

Wes directed them with hand signals, in order not to startle the cattle. Gradually the three of them managed to pull the cattle into a compact group and moved them down the slopes into the small valley that fed into the larger one where the camp was located.

When they reached the camp, they discovered the herd had tripled in their absence. With the cattle they had found, they were already close to seventy head of cattle. Rosemary was greatly cheered to already have that number on the first day.

Wes, however, after talking with Cookie, discovered the trio that included Ted still had not shown up.

"You two grab some lunch. I'm going to go check on that group. I'm hoping they're not in trouble."

"Wes, you need some lunch, too," Rosemary protested.

"Then see what Cookie has that I can take with me."

Rosemary hastily made a quick sandwich and handed it to him. "Give me your canteen and I'll fill it quickly."

After she handed it back to him, she opened her mouth, but he spoke first. "I know, be careful. I promise."

Jason stared after him. "I think I should go with him. Ted is my responsibility."

"Yes, we could do without Ted, but Wes will take care of everything," Rosemary said.

"We don't know that he's caused any difficulties today," Jason said stubbornly.

"How much do you want to bet?" Rosemary returned, anger in her voice.

"You need to eat some lunch and take a break, so you'll be ready to go out again when Wes gets back." He turned to Cookie. "Shall we fix sandwiches?"

"Naw, I've got a casserole ready to eat. Just serve yourselves. It's over there by the fire."

Jason got two plates and filled them both, handing one to Rosemary who was still staring in the direction Wes had gone.

"Thank you." She looked down. "Oh, you made the green enchilada recipe, Cookie! It's one of my favorites."

"I know," Cookie said with a grin.

"I don't think I've had this before," Jason said, studying it. "Is it hot?"

"No, it's not. The green peppers in it aren't jalapeños."

They ate their lunch, but Wes still hadn't come back.

"What do we do now?" Rosemary said almost to herself.

"You stay here. I'm going to look for all of them." Jason moved toward his horse.

"No! I'm going with you. It's a mistake for anyone to go on their own. Anything could happen."

She swung into the saddle and gathered her reins. Jason was staring at her and she said, "Well? Aren't you ready?"

"I really think you should stay here."

"No, I'm not going to. You can stay if you want." Then she urged her horse toward the direction Wes had taken. Jason immediately reached her side and rode with her.

"Are you always this hardheaded?" he asked.

"Always," she drawled and kept up the pace, her eyes scanning the countryside, looking for any sign of her ranch manager or the three men who were supposed to be in this area.

After almost forty-five minutes, they pulled up. "Could we have missed them?" Rosemary asked.

"No." Jason pointed to some movement a distance away. They weren't sure if it was the riders or some animals. But they got closer and were able to see some riders.

"How many can you see?" Rosemary asked anxiously.

"Only three, but I think that's Wes's black gelding on the right."

Rosemary prayed Jason was right. She wanted to speed up, but the terrain was too rough.

"What could've gone wrong?" Jason asked.

"A million different things. Wait! I think one of them is leading a fourth horse. Oh, no!"

Jason moved forward in front of Rosemary. "You should wait here until I find out what's up."

"No, I'm coming with you. I'm not going to get hysterical!" Unless Wes was hurt. That would undo her. Especially now after her father's death.

As they grew closer, Rosemary was sure that was Wes on his black gelding. Jason managed to pick out Ted, and Rosemary thought the other man was Rafe, an older cowboy. But where was Jesse, the third cowboy in the group?

Finally they got close enough to discover Jesse was on a hand-made stretcher tied between Wes and Rafe. Ted was the one leading the extra horse.

Jason reached over and caught Rosemary's reins. "Let's wait for them here."

"Why?"

"There's not much room up there. We'll do better to stay here and not crowd them. Carrying that stretcher between two horses isn't easy."

"I feel so bad for Jesse," Rosemary said softly.

"We all do. I'd guess Wes is already figuring out what to do to help him."

"Cookie is our medic. He used to work as an EMT in Cheyenne. But he wanted to cook."

Jason grinned. "That's a strange combination of talents."

"It comes in handy," Rosemary replied, "especially at times like this."

"Maybe the best thing would be to go back and alert Cookie. You could do that while I wait for them."

"Why should I go and not you?" She was getting tired of Jason treating her as if she was a porcelain doll.

Jason gave her a sideways smile. "Because I'm stronger if they need someone to spell them."

"I think the horses are doing all the work!"

"I think they're putting a lot of muscle in it."

The man never gave up, she had to admit. She surrendered. "Okay, okay, I'll go warn Cookie." She cast Jesse another glance. "Do you think he's broken his leg?"

"Just go tell Cookie they're bringing in someone on a stretcher."

"All right."

"You won't lose your way back to the camp, will you?"

She heard the teasing in his voice and gave him a mock glare. Then she pulled Maggie's head around and started back to camp to alert Cookie of his change in jobs.

"How is he?" Jason asked Wes as he rode alongside the manager.

"I think he has a concussion. He hit his head and passed out for a few minutes, according to Rafe."

"Concussions are dangerous."

"Oh, yeah. That's why we tied him between the two horses. If we'd dragged him behind on the stretcher, he might not've made it back to camp."

"How did it happen?" Jason asked, his voice even lower.

"We'll talk later," Wes whispered.

Jason frowned and looked back at Ted, riding behind them, showing no concern at all. He pulled back on the reins to wait until Ted came up beside him.

"What happened?"

"How would I know? I'm no damned baby-sitter."

Jason frowned. He'd really made a mistake with Ted. That bothered him. Had his excitement about getting the ranch made him less perceptive than he usually was about people? He didn't know, but he intended to get rid of Ted as soon as they got back to town. He couldn't fire him here. It would be too awkward.

He rode silently behind the men with the

rough stretcher, wondering how good Cookie was at handling head wounds.

When they reached the camp, Cookie was there, waiting for them, with Rosemary at his side. "How is he?" Cookie asked.

Wes swung down from his horse. "He hasn't said much, and it hasn't come out right. I think we're going to need to get him to a hospital pretty damn quick."

Cookie was looking at Jesse's eyes. "Yeah, you're right. But I don't know how to get him there without doing more damage. Even if I drove him there, I'd bounce him all over the place."

"How about a helicopter?" Jason suggested.

Everyone turned to stare at him. "Wouldn't that cost a lot?" Wes asked.

"I'm willing to pay for it. Will my cell phone work out here?"

"Yes, I think so. We're just north of Rock Springs," Rosemary said.

"Okay, I'll call my secretary and see what she can arrange." Jason pulled his cell phone out of his saddlebag and moved away from the others to make his call. When he'd made the arrangements, he turned to Wes. "It'll be here in an hour. I think we should move the cattle ahead so they won't scatter when the copter lands."

"Good thinking. We'll leave Jesse here with Cookie and Rosemary. That okay with you, Rosie?"

"Yes, I'll stay here with Jesse," Rosemary promised, holding the man's hand.

Jason frowned. Did all the cowboys have a crush on Rosemary?

He pulled Wes aside. "Maybe you should warn Rosie about not making promises to Jesse that she thinks will help him get well."

Wes frowned. "What are you talking about?"

"Well, she's holding Jesse's hand, and she might—I mean, I just think you should warn her."

Wes grinned. "Yeah, I'll do that."

Wes moved to Rosie's side and drew her apart. Jason didn't know exactly what Wes said, but Rosie flashed him an angry look.

Before he could get close enough to talk to her, Wes ordered everyone to mount up so they could move the herd forward about half a mile.

"What did you say to Rosie?" Jason asked as soon as he rode up beside Wes.

"I told her you were concerned about her

promising anything to Jesse to help him get well. Isn't that what you said?"

"Yeah, but she looked angrily at me, like I'd done something wrong."

"She thought you were being… Let's see, I think the word she used was ridiculous."

"Well, thanks, Wes, that'll help a lot," Jason said in disgust.

"I know," Wes said with a grin.

"Hey, is someone going to fly to the hospital with Jesse? I hadn't thought about that."

"No. I'm going to call Sara Beth and have her meet them at the hospital. I need to keep all the able riders here so we can get this roundup done."

"Sara Beth won't mind?"

"Naw, she's used to helping out."

"You two make a good team," Jason said with a smile.

"Yeah. I miss her." After a moment of silence when Wes was clearly thinking of his wife, he looked at Jason. "What about you? You got a special lady back in Denver?"

Jason reared back in surprise. "Me? Hell, no! Denver ladies aren't interested in living on a ranch. They want to be where they think the action is. I'm tired of that kind of life."

"You mean parties and things like that?" Wes asked.

"Yeah. A lot of people go from one party to another and don't do anything productive with their lives. And there are women who lock onto a man who can provide their needs so they can be on the party circuit."

"You sound like it's something you've experienced personally," Wes said.

"Yeah. I was married to one of those women. I don't ever want to be caught in that trap again."

"I was afraid Rosie wouldn't want to leave Cheyenne and come back to the ranch, but she didn't hesitate. Her dad had talked her into going to Cheyenne because he didn't want her to know that he was too tired to do what had to be done. But if he'd let her come home, she would've stopped the slide."

"That's a shame. Is that why he sold the ranch without talking to her?"

"I think he was ashamed that he'd let things go so badly and because he was so tired, which the doc said was caused by his heart disease. I also think he didn't believe he was going to live much longer. I've heard sometimes people who are ill know when death is coming."

"Yeah. He seemed like a nice man, but I could tell something was wrong. But you and Sara Beth are willing to stay if I get the ranch, right?"

"Sure, as long as you don't mind if Rosie comes to visit from time to time."

"No, I wouldn't mind that." Jason pulled his hat lower, hoping Wes wouldn't be able to read the emotion in his eyes.

"I hear the 'copter!" one of the lead cowboys yelled, pointing into the sky.

Both Wes and Jason paused and watched the copter fly over.

"It should reach the SUV in about five minutes," Wes muttered.

"Yeah," Jason agreed, his mind on the woman waiting for the helicopter.

"You know what I think?" Wes asked.

Shaken from his thoughts of Rosemary, Jason turned to look at Wes. "No, I don't. What do you think?"

"I think Nick's not the only one who has Rosie on the brain."

CHAPTER FOUR

THE rest of the day, after Jesse's dramatic departure, consisted of rounding up cattle. Jason avoided Wes, and Rosemary avoided him. Which was difficult since they were supposed to be a team.

Ted also seemed to be into avoidance. Every time Jason got close to him, he scattered in a different direction. Finally Jason decided he had to talk to Wes. He wanted to know what had happened up on that trail.

"Wes, hold up a minute. I need to ask you what happened to Jesse up there. He's not a new rider, so how did he fall?"

"I asked Rafe, but he couldn't tell me for sure, Jason. He said he'd been in the lead when he heard a yell. He turned around to see Jesse on the ground. The strange thing was, Ted was almost beside him when they'd been riding single-file."

Jason wanted to jump to the conclusion that Ted had shoved Jesse off his horse, but he couldn't really believe that even Ted would do something that blatant. "I'll ask Ted about it," he promised.

"Yeah, that'd be a good idea."

When they rode in for dinner was the first time Jason had to talk to his once-future ranch manager. "Ted?"

"Yeah, Jason?" the man answered as he unsaddled his horse.

"What happened up there with Jesse?"

"I told you I'm not a damned baby-sitter. I wasn't watching him. For some reason, he fell off his horse. Maybe he fell asleep. We're not getting all that much sleep up here."

Jason frowned. His suggestion sounded reasonable. He couldn't outright accuse Ted of shoving Jesse from the saddle. He put his horse in the rope corral and carried his saddle near the SUV so he could bed down beside Wes and Rosemary as he had the past two nights.

Then, as he usually did, he located Rosemary. He liked to know where she was. For her safety, of course.

When she got in line for dinner, he fell in behind her. "I sure am hungry tonight."

She glared at him over her shoulder but said nothing.

"We've got a pretty good-size herd already. I'm surprised."

"Because you thought I was lying to you in Denver?" she asked.

"Well, not lying, exactly, but I thought you might've expanded your hopes a little."

Her jaw tightened and she completely turned her back to him. That was all right. He planned on sitting next to her while they ate.

He followed her from the fire to take the canvas seat next to her. Then he said in a low voice, "Ted said he thought Jesse fell asleep in the saddle and that's why he fell."

"Jesse is an experienced cowboy. He knows the risks, and there's no way he fell asleep!" Rosemary said in heated tones.

Jason didn't say anything for a minute. When he was sure no one was watching them, he said, "I didn't say I believed him, but without any proof, I can't accuse him of anything."

"You don't *want* to accuse him!"

"Rosie, I don't want him going around doing bad things to honest cowboys. That wouldn't be fair."

"I know that. But you're letting him remain here, when we don't need him!"

"So you think I should send him away?"

"Of course I do. Even if nothing is his fault, I'm going to blame it on him because he's the outsider. If we weren't sleeping right next to the SUV, I feel sure he'd try to puncture one of Cookie's tires."

"I hadn't thought of that. I'll try to keep an eye on him."

"Does that mean you'll be riding out with him instead of with Wes and me in the morning?"

"Is that what you want?" he asked, staring at her.

She shrugged her shoulders. "Doesn't matter to me! But you'd better warn Wes. He'll need to reorganize if you are."

"I'd rather stay with you and Wes."

"Why?" she quickly demanded.

"Because Wes knows so much. I'm learning a lot from him."

Apparently his answer wasn't what she expected. "Oh." After a minute, she said, "I think Wes and I can manage on our own."

"I don't think Sara Beth would think so."

"Why not?" she asked, her voice stiff with anger.

"Because if something happened to Wes, you'd have trouble getting him back to camp. You're a skilled horsewoman, and I know you're a crack shot, but it would take muscle to get Wes back to camp. That's where I come in."

"So you want me to ride out with Ted?"

"No, I don't want you to ride out with anyone other than Wes. And me."

"I can take care of myself!"

"And that's why Wes always takes you with him?"

"Not always! Sometimes I ride with Rafe and whoever his partner is. But not Ted. I don't want a concussion."

Wes joined them, sitting on Rosemary's other side. "You two need to learn to whisper, especially if you're talking about something that could turn this campsite into a big brawl," he said.

"If we whisper, they'll think something else is going on!" Rosemary protested.

"So? We'd survive that, Rosie, but not an accusation of someone hurting Jesse on purpose. We don't have any proof that any such thing happened."

"I think it would be better if Jason sat with someone else," Rosemary said stubbornly.

"But I prefer your company," Jason returned.

She glared at him.

"Rosie, put a lid on it," Wes ordered her. "We've all got to appear friendly until this roundup is over."

That comment hit Jason where it hurt. He asked Wes, "You mean you won't work for me when the roundup is over? If I get the ranch, I mean."

"Of course I will. It's my home, mine and Sara Beth's. She won't want to leave."

"You had me worried there for a minute."

"But we don't want any arguments breaking out amongst us. So you two keep a civil tongue in your heads."

"Fine!" Rosemary snapped.

"I'm not the one being difficult," Jason said, smiling at Wes.

"That's sure not the way to make her happy, Jason. Give her some space and some time. Remember what I told you."

That night as they were getting ready for bed, Rosemary whispered to Wes, "What did you tell Jason?"

"Only that this was a hard time for you, what

with your daddy dying and the question about losing the ranch. That's all. It's true, isn't it? You're a bit more prickly than I've ever seen you."

"I'm sorry, Wes," she said with a sigh. "I guess that's what it is."

"I understand, honey. But Jason isn't the enemy. Even if he gets the ranch, he won't mind you coming to visit us. I asked him."

Rosemary's eyes filled with tears. "I—I can't think about that!" Then she turned her back on Wes and snuggled down in her sleeping bag.

It sounded to her that Wes might prefer for Jason to get the ranch. After all, he'd have plenty of money to fix it up to the standards Wes liked to maintain. And it was obvious Jason would be a good owner to work for. Wes and Sara Beth would be secure.

That was something to be grateful for, she supposed, but it would shut her out. She would no longer have the ranch, and she wasn't sure she could come see it, or Wes and Sara Beth. Not with Jason around.

Her eyes filled with tears again and she determinedly shut them. She would not cry on the roundup. Everyone would be trying to comfort her and looking for someone to blame. She didn't want that, any more than Wes did.

Her father had told her she could come on the roundups as long as she didn't act like a girl. Any tears and he'd send her home at once. She hadn't really believed him. But she'd had enough doubt not to test him.

Finally exhaustion shut out her tears and she fell asleep.

Until about three in the morning, when lightning ruptured the dark of the night and thunder awakened her.

Wes was already sitting up in his sleeping bag, staring up at the sky. Then he pulled on his coat and boots. He went around the campfire, wakening each cowboy and giving him instructions. Some of them raced to the horse corral to saddle up, while others rolled up their bags and headed for the dual cab of the SUV where Cookie slept.

Then he returned to her side. "Put your sleeping bag under the SUV, Rosie. I think we're going to have a big rainstorm."

"No, I'll ride with you, Wes. I can help."

"I'm counting on you helping in the morning, honey. I'll need some sleep then.

You'll be in charge. Now get on under there before the heavens open up."

The SUV had oversize tires that gave her plenty of clearance. She'd slept there before in a rainstorm. She got out of her sleeping bag and shoved it under the SUV, as Wes had suggested, but she was shocked when Jason did the same.

"What are you doing?" she demanded in a harsh whisper.

"I'm doing what Wes told me to do," Jason replied.

"I don't believe you!"

"Wes?" Jason called. When Wes appeared, having bent down so he could see their faces, Jason said, "Rosemary doesn't believe you told me to sleep under here."

"Of course I did, Rosie. Don't be foolish. You both need to sleep and there's no more room in the cab. You'll both stay dry under there. And I'm counting on Jason to keep an eye on you."

Then he disappeared.

Rosemary scooted over so there was room for Jason. "I need my saddle and coat," she said.

Jason scooted out and retrieved those for

her and then got his own. He helped her put her coat on the saddle as a pillow, then he settled down beside her.

"Will we stay dry?" he asked.

"We should. The others stored their saddles under the back end of the SUV and draped a waterproof tarp over that end. It keeps some wood dry for the fire in the morning, too." On cue, the rain began to fall. It wasn't a gentle rain. The drops were like pellets striking the metal of the truck as if they'd been fired out of a rifle.

She shuddered, and Jason leaned closer. "Are you afraid of storms?"

"A—a little. My dad used to tease me if I showed any fear, so I've always tried to hide it, but—" She stopped herself. Why was she making such a confession to Jason?

She felt him scoot a little closer in the dark. "Wes told me to keep you safe."

"I'm not going to make a fuss."

"I know. But maybe we could hold hands, just to feel the contact of someone else here."

She was hesitant. Her father had been so strict about her not acting like a girl. "I guess we could—as long as you'll treat me just like another cowboy in the morning."

"I promise. This is just for thunderstorms."

"All right." She turned to face Jason and stuck her hand out of the sleeping bag.

He took her hand and carried it to his lips.

She snatched her hand back. "What are you doing?"

"I was afraid to ask for a good-night kiss," he whispered. "I don't think I damaged it any. Come on, give it back to me."

After a moment, Rosemary extended her hand again. It was enveloped in the warmth of his hand. He scooted even closer, until their breaths were mixed.

"Are you cold?" she whispered.

"No, I just enjoy being close during a thunderstorm."

She could hear his smile, even if she couldn't see it in the dark. "Are you making fun of me?"

"No. Just go back to sleep, sweetheart. It will be morning soon."

Rosemary took his advice. Surprisingly she felt comforted by the warmth of his hand. Her eyes slowly shut and she drifted off to sleep.

Jason came awake slowly the next morning. He didn't hear the comforting sounds of

Cookie preparing breakfast. All he heard was the rain. But he was still holding Rosie's hand. He again carried it to his lips for a silent kiss.

Should he get out in the rain and mount up to go help the other cowboys? Was it the closing of the SUV's doors that awakened him? He peered out from under the SUV, but he didn't see any movement.

He looked at Rosie. She was sleeping on her side, turned toward him, her cheeks flushed with warmth. He'd never seen her look so sweet and adorable. That was a strange thought coming from him, he decided. He hadn't thought of any woman as sweet and adorable. Sexy, maybe, as Rosie was, but she looked vulnerable this morning.

He lay back down deciding there was no sudden need for him to wake up. He could lie beside Rosie and watch her sleep. Mindful of duty, he checked his watch. It was after eight. The men who had gone out at three were probably exhausted.

Though reluctant, he let go of Rosie's hand and sat up a little to pull on his coat, trying not to move any more than necessary. He didn't want Rosie thinking she had to get out in the rain. He immediately worried about leaving her alone. Wes had told him to stay with her until he came back in.

He decided it would be all right if he woke Rosie and told her where he was going. She could stay under the truck as long as she was awake.

Life wasn't quite that simple when it involved Rosie.

"What?" she mumbled when he shook her slightly.

"Honey, I'm going out to help Wes. You should stay here, but I wanted you to be awake so you could protect yourself if you need to."

Her eyes flew open. "What? What are you talking about? It's still raining!" She looked at her watch. "Good heavens! We overslept. We should've relieved Wes two hours ago."

Before Jason could say anything, she had her coat on and was reaching for her boots.

"Rosie, you should stay here. We can't get breakfast until Cookie can start a fire, so just —"

By then she had her boots on and her slicker draped over one arm as scooted to the edge of the SUV. She slapped her hat on her head to keep the rain off as soon as she cleared the truck.

"Are you coming?" she called.

"I'm right behind you," Jason told her, but actually he came out on the other side of the truck.

Rosemary was banging on the windows of the SUV, waking up the cowboys inside. She pointed to her watch and hurried toward the rope corral after putting on her slicker and retrieving her saddle. Jason joined her and had their horses saddled as the other cowboys emerged from the truck.

"We're heading out," she told them. "Join us as soon as you can. Once it stops raining, we'll take turns coming in for a quick breakfast."

Then she swung into the saddle and headed toward the area where they kept the herd.

Unfortunately, when they got there, they didn't find the herd, or any riders. The rain was coming down in sheets, and Rosie was so upset that Jason immediately tried to send her back to the camp. But being Rosie, she refused.

"We've got to find them. The rain was blowing southwest to northeast, so that's the direction the cattle would've gone." Without another word, she headed in that direction.

Jason realized he would lose sight of her in

the rain, even with her yellow slicker on, if he didn't keep up with her.

They rode in silence for a few minutes. He could sense the serious concern on her mind. If nothing else, she was worried about Wes. And then there was the herd. It was her ticket to the recovery of her ranch.

Hearing a sound in the distance, he stopped his horse. Rosemary turned to stare at him, pulling to a stop also.

"I heard something," he said. Then the sound of a cow mooing came again. "We're on the right track. Just keep going."

Five minutes later, they caught up with the remnants of the herd. They had lost more than half of the cattle. Rosemary rode around the herd, checking with each of the men. Jason followed along behind her, acknowledging each of the men as they went by. When they'd made the complete circle, Rosie wheeled her horse around.

"Where's Wes?" When he looked at her blankly, she rode to the nearest rider to ask that question again.

It didn't take long to realize none of the men knew Wes's whereabouts. She told them to move the herd back in the direction of the camp. Then she started out ahead. Jason wheeled around and caught up with her. "What are we looking for?"

"Wes's horse would never leave him. Look for the horse. That's where we'll find Wes."

After half an hour in the torrential rain, Rosemary spotted Wes's horse. She swung down from the saddle, letting her reins drag the ground in a silent command to her well-trained horse. Maggie stood still as Rosie searched for Wes. Through the rain she couldn't see anything. "Wes? Wes, where are you?" she called.

Jason dismounted, too. "Did you hear any response?"

"No, and I'm not sure I would with the rain and all." She moved away, trying to find Wes. Suddenly she disappeared from Jason's view.

He panicked. "Rosie? Rosie? Where are you?"

"Be careful, Jason. There's a drop-off. I'm okay, I just— Wes? I think I've found Wes."

"Okay, I'm coming down." Jason found the edge where the land fell away. Sliding down, he found himself almost on top of Rosie. She helped him stand.

"Wes is over here. I don't know how we'll get him up to the horses."

Jason bent down. The man was soaked and cold, but he was a welcome sight. "Wes, how you doing?"

"I think I broke my ankle. I haven't been able to get up."

"Could you stand to be dragged out by my horse? I'm not sure how we'll get you to the top if we don't."

"I figured."

"Okay, Rosie, I'm going up to get the rope off my horse. I'll toss it down to you. Tie it around his chest, under his arms. Then holler up to me and I'll have Shadow pull him up."

"Okay."

Jason did as he said and stood waiting for Rosie to let him know they were ready. When he didn't hear anything, he called down. "Rosie? What's happening?"

"Sorry. Wes had to tell me how to tie it. I think he's ready, but go slow."

"Will do." He began backing his horse up slowly, inch by inch. They only had to get Wes up about eight feet but the going seemed endless. Finally Wes's head popped into view, and Jason knew they were almost done. Rosie climbed over the rim, intent only on helping Wes.

"Wes, are you okay" she asked as the ranch manager lay on the ground, trying to remove the rope by himself.

"Rosie," he croaked. "Thank God you found me. Thanks to you, too, Jason. I thought I was going to die out here."

By that time, Jason was beside the duo to help Wes take the rope off. "Are you hurt anywhere beside your ankle?"

"Naw." He let out a swear. "Something knocked me from my horse. I landed awkwardly and broke my ankle. And then I rolled down into that hole. I didn't think anyone would find me."

Rosie was already looking at his ankle. "It's swollen badly. We're going to have to cut your boot to get it off."

"We've got to get him back to camp first." Jason wondered aloud if they'd have to make a litter for Wes, but the older man told them no.

"I can ride in if you'll help me get up on my horse."

"It'll swell up even more, Wes," Rosemary protested.

"Rosie, if I don't get to camp soon, I'll die of hypothermia. We'll tend to my ankle once we get there."

His words spurred Rosemary and Jason to quick action. Since his right ankle was broken, Jason helped him get his left foot in the stirrup and he swung his right foot over the saddle. They could see the pain on his face, but they thought it was the best way to get him to safety.

Within fifteen minutes, they got him to camp. The rain was tapering to a slow drizzle by that time. Cookie was building a fire with the dry wood he'd hidden under the SUV. No one else was in camp.

When they got Wes to the fire, Jason caught him in his arms as he slid off his horse. "Tend to the horses, Rosie. I'll get him to the SUV. Cookie!" Jason shouted, which got the man's attention. "We think he has a broken ankle. It's badly swollen and he's frozen. We need to warm him up quickly and cut his boot off."

The two men got Wes into the back seat of the SUV, covered him with the sleeping bags the cowboys had left in the cab. Then Cookie got a butcher knife and slit the side of Wes's boot until he could ease it off his foot.

Rosemary stood there, peering over Cookie's shoulder, holding her breath.

"Rosie, I got the coffeepot put on. Go see if

it's perked and get the boss a cup of hot coffee."

Rosemary immediately followed Cookie's order.

"How bad is it?" Jason asked as Cookie closed the truck door to give Wes some rest.

He shook his head. "Not good. He may need surgery."

"Want me to get the helicopter back out here?"

"Let's wait on that. After we warm him up, I'll talk to the boss and decide what to do."

Rosemary appeared with a cup of coffee for Wes, which Cookie took from her.

"I'll give it to him, Rosie. You and Jason go get some coffee. It's going to be a few minutes until he's ready to talk to you."

"But he's going to be all right, isn't he?" Rosemary asked anxiously.

"Yeah, he'll be fine."

"Come on, Rosie, let's let Cookie take care of him." He turned to the man. "Maybe you should put a slug of whiskey in his coffee to dull the pain, if you've got any."

"I do, for medicinal purposes only. But this definitely calls for it."

With a grin, Jason led Rosie back to the fire.

After pouring them both cups of coffee, he said, "He's going to be all right, Rosie. You found him in time. Once he gets warmed up, he'll be in a lot of pain, but I can call out the helicopter again. We'll take care of him."

It was the tin cup rattling against Rosemary's teeth that alerted Jason to the state she was in. He took the coffee from her and set both cups down on a nearby rock. Then he wrapped his arms around her. "Rosie? Did you hear me? He's going to be all right."

But Rosie merely stood there, staring ahead and shaking. She said nothing.

When Jason pulled her in his arms, Rosemary hid her face against his chest, unwilling to face the fact that Wes had been hurt and wouldn't be able to continue the roundup. She was going to have to be strong enough to do it on her own.

And pray that Wes would be all right.

She'd been so afraid he was dead when she'd first found him in that hole, unmoving. If that had been true, she wouldn't have been able to go on.

All she could think was that he'd left her—the way her father had left her, and her mother before him. And she'd have let down Sara Beth, who'd asked her to watch her husband.

When her mother died, one of the last things she'd said to Rosemary was "Take care of your father." Rosie had done her best; she'd tried. But Robert Wilson was a stubborn, prideful man. He didn't allow anyone to fuss over him, though Sara Beth liked to think she did. Several years later he'd sent Rosie away to Cheyenne to work, and she'd had to be content with phone calls and visits.

In truth, she'd seen her father's decline over the last couple of years, but he wouldn't allow her help. Sometimes, when the grief overcame her, she felt guilty for not trying harder.

Whether or not she'd let her parents down, she'd determined she wouldn't do the same for her surrogate parents, Wes and Sara Beth. But seeing Wes lying there, unmoving, was like a flashback to her father, and all the guilt, all the sadness, came storming back.

Thankfully he'd been alive, and Jason had helped her get him back to camp.

"He's going to be fine," Jason repeated, as if knowing she needed to hear the words again and again.

He cuddled her against him, letting his

warmth help her accept his words. It helped, just as his hand-holding last night had helped.

But she had to be strong. And she hoped she could be strong enough. Her future depended on it.

CHAPTER FIVE

"I WANT to know what happened."

Jason looked up at the sound of Rosie's voice. They'd been sitting in silence around the campfire for the last half hour, drinking hot coffee to warm themselves while Cookie tended Wes. Every time he'd tried to engage her in conversation, she'd ignored him. Apparently now she was ready to talk.

"There's no way Wes could've just fallen off his horse, Jason, so don't even try that excuse again." She turned and glared at him. "Something's going on around here and I'm going to find out what!"

Jason agreed with Rosemary, and he knew just where to start. With Ted. But first he had to talk to Wes and find out what happened.

Of course, he couldn't convince Rosemary to wait by the fire. She followed him to the SUV. "I want to see Wes."

"I don't think he's ready for visitors," Cookie said, "especially female visitors. I had to remove his jeans," Cookie explained.

"He's covered up, isn't he?" Rosemary demanded.

"Yeah, but he's gone to sleep now that he's warm. He needs his rest."

"I know, but it's important, Cookie. We need to know what happened."

Jason looked at the stubbornness on her face and, with a sigh, nodded to Cookie. "I think she's right, Cookie. This is the second accident in two days. We need to figure out what's going on."

"Okay. I'll try to wake him."

After several minutes, Cookie had aroused Wes. Jason leaned forward. "Wes, we need to know what happened."

Wes frowned, as if thinking was difficult. "I…fell off my horse when…someone rode by me and shoved me. I landed wrong."

"Who pushed you off your horse? Did you see?"

"He—he wore a black slicker. I thought everyone was wearing a yellow one."

Jason frowned. He didn't know what color slicker Ted wore, because he hadn't gone with the others in the middle of the night. But he intended to find out.

"Let him sleep now," Cookie ordered.

Rosemary backed away and turned to Jason. "Well? What color does Ted wear?"

"I don't know. We'll have to wait until the men who got up early come in. It shouldn't be too long."

"If it's Ted, I want to have him arrested. First Jesse and now Wes. That's unacceptable."

"I understand. If it's Ted, I'll get rid of him. If you want to have him arrested, I'm all for it."

"Good!" Rosemary exclaimed and moved back to the campfire, sticking her hands out to feel the warmth. They both sat by the fire until they heard horses approaching. It was still drizzling, so all the men wore slickers—except Ted. Rosemary and Jason exchanged a look.

"Don't worry, I'll find out," Jason said.

He moved toward the corral where the men would leave their horses. When Ted got off his horse, loudly complaining about the conditions and not getting enough sleep, Jason stopped him.

"You look pretty wet, Ted. Didn't you bring a slicker?"

"Nope, I forgot it. But I'll dry out by the fire."

"It seems a little strange that you wouldn't bring a slicker," Jason persisted.

Nick, having put his horse in the corral, was walking to the fire when he overheard Jason and Ted. "He had a slicker on earlier. Didn't you, Ted?"

"No, I didn't have a slicker," Ted protested.

"What color was his slicker?" Jason asked.

"It was black. It made it hard for us to see him." Nick didn't continue to the fire. He seemed to realize something important was going down.

"You pushed Wes from his saddle, didn't you, Ted?" Jason asked.

Nick's head jerked and he stared at Jason. "The boss is hurt?"

"Yeah. He broke his ankle when someone in a black slicker pushed him off his horse."

Nick immediately charged Ted, but Jason stepped in between the two men. "Take it easy, Nick. He's not getting away with it. Can you help me?"

"Sure, if it means getting rid of him!"

"Get your rifle and come guard him. And if he even thinks about getting up, shoot him in the arm or leg. I don't really care which."

Nick hurried off to get his rifle.

"Do you hear that, Ted? You're to sit here by the fire and wait for me to decide what we're doing with you."

Ted seemed unfazed. "You don't have any proof! Besides, I'll tell everyone you hired me to do the dirty deeds so you could get the ranch."

"No one will believe you," Jason returned.

"Yes, they will. You're not part of this group any more than I am!"

"I'll take my chances. Just sit down and stay put."

Jason stared at him, until Ted looked away. By then, Nick was back with his rifle and he took a seat close to Ted, practically growling at him.

Jason, followed by Rosemary, went back to the SUV. "I need to talk to Wes," he told Cookie.

"You want to wake him up again?" Cookie asked sternly. "I don't think that's a good idea."

"I need to know about the helicopter. Is he willing to go back like that?"

"He'd better be. That's the best thing. I've made a splint for his ankle, but it's a bad break." He opened the door to the backseat.

Jason leaned in. "Wes, are you awake?"

"Yeah," Wes muttered, not opening his eyes.

"Is it okay to send for the helicopter again? It's the best way to get you back to the ranch."

That made Wes open his eyes. "No! I'm not going in the helicopter! That thing scares me to death!" His voice sounded rusty, as if he hadn't used it in a long while, but the emotion in his voice rang true.

"But, Wes, you've got to get to the hospital!" Rosemary said, inching in beside Jason. "I don't know how you'll get back to town without the helicopter."

"I'll get there the same way I came," he growled.

"But you can't let your leg hang down. It'll swell up too much," Cookie said from the front seat.

"Then I'll ride sidesaddle with my ankle held horizontally. If ladies can do it, I sure can!"

"Wes, you're being stubborn," Rosemary argued. "Sara Beth wouldn't approve of you riding back to the house when you could go by helicopter. It would take about eighteen hours to get to the house."

"I'm not going in the helicopter," he said as if that was the final word on the subject.

"How about I send Rafe with you, to make sure you get there?" Jason suggested. "And he can take Ted with him. Ted's the one who pushed you off your horse, Wes. He probably did the same thing to Jesse. I want to get him away from here. When we get back, I'll deal with him."

"Good," Wes said. "Yeah, Rafe will be good, but it'll leave you short of riders."

"We'll manage," he assured Wes. "You just focus on getting better. Cookie says you may have to have surgery."

Wes scowled. "Maybe I'll get a walking cast. I can't stay in the hospital long. I've got to help Rosie take care of things."

"I'll be all right, Wes," Rosemary promised. "I need to know that you're getting help. And with Ted gone, we'll manage better, I promise."

"And you'll let Jason help you?"

Rosemary glanced at the man standing beside her. He was big and strong, and she knew she had no choice. "Yes, Wes, I will."

Wes relaxed a little. "Okay, now run along while I talk to Jason."

"Why do you have to talk to Jason in private? You can tell me anything," Rosemary insisted.

Jason turned to her. "Rosie, Wes wants to tell me to take care of you. So go away so neither of us will be embarrassed."

"I'm not embarrassed. I want to know what he's going to say!"

"Rosie— Okay. I want a promise from Jason that he won't take advantage of you. Understand?"

"I promise, Wes," Jason said. "I'll take care of her and we'll be back to the ranch on time with the herd."

"Okay," Wes said. Then he switched subjects. "Cookie, we'll need to leave about five in the morning, and we'll need some lunch and maybe a snack to get us to the ranch."

"Are you sure you can make it in one day?" Rosie asked.

"We'll make it. We'll ride until we get there. Unlike here, the pastures are free of rocks, so if we ride after dark, we won't hurt the horses."

"That's true," Jason agreed, "but are you sure your body will hold up that long, in the strained position you'll be in?"

"I'll make it. Where's Rafe?"

"I think he's catching up on some sleep. We didn't tell anyone about your accident until we could find out who was responsible." Jason didn't bother telling him about Nick, who was guarding Ted.

"But I didn't see the man's face," Wes said.

"We're sure it was Ted. Don't worry about it," Jason assured him. "Now we'll let you get some more sleep."

He pulled Rosemary away from the SUV, even though she didn't want to go with him.

"What are you doing?" she asked. "I want to talk to Wes again!"

"We need to let him sleep so he'll be able to make the trip tomorrow. And you need to work with Cookie to make sure they have plenty of food for their trip."

"And you need to stop telling me what to do. I know my responsibilities. Of course I'll help Cookie, but first I think I can talk Wes into riding in the helicopter. If I can just—"

Without warning Jason leaned over and kissed her soft lips.

She jerked away, shocked, and stared at him. "Wh-what are you doing?"

"Shutting you up the only way I know how." He stood his ground, trying to gauge her reaction. She sputtered a few times but at least she didn't smack him. When he figured it was safe, he said in a soft voice, "There's no point in talking to Wes about the 'copter. I think he's afraid to fly. Has he done it before?"

"I—I don't think so. But—"

"Then you'll only embarrass him. He doesn't want to admit that he's afraid. If he keeps his ankle up, he'll make it home and not be embarrassed."

"Did Cookie agree?" Rosemary asked, a bit calmer now.

"Yeah, I believe he did. Now, why don't you go plan what to fix for them?"

Rosemary gave him a hard stare. "Are you trying to get rid of me?"

"I'd never want to do that, honey. But the food will be important if they're going to get there safely."

"All right, but I don't think I want to fix any food for Ted!"

"That's up to you, Rosie. If you can live with not giving him any food, I won't protest."

Rosemary stood there. "Oh, you make me so mad! You know I can't be that mean. But that's what he deserves."

"Yeah, it is."

Jason stood there watching her stomp off, outraged by her own goodness. She was the most interesting woman he'd ever met. Tough, spirited, loyal…and beautiful.

Rosie Wilson may not be perfect, but she was the closest thing to it he'd ever seen.

Rosemary worked out with Cookie what to prepare for Wes, Rafe and Ted. They would eat breakfast before they left early in the morning, so she packed up lunch and dinner along with some cookies.

She decided she'd call Sara Beth tomorrow to tell her Wes was coming. She could take one of the other trucks and ride out to meet them. The land was too rough where they were for one of their regular trucks to make the drive, but the land closer to the ranch house wasn't as bad. Rosemary knew how worried Sara Beth would be. She could drive her husband straight to the hospital.

But Rosemary wouldn't tell Wes what she was going to do. He would fuss at her, tell her he didn't need Sara Beth to meet him. But by tomorrow afternoon, he'd welcome that truck.

She had a sinking feeling in her stomach about the rest of the roundup, too. She would be in charge, along with Jason. The task was daunting, and so much was at stake.

With Wes gone, they would all have to work together to accomplish the goals. They would now be four men short. Cookie wouldn't be working the cattle, so that would leave ten cowboys, including her and Jason. Two would tend the cattle they'd collected, until the herd grew larger. That would leave eight people to go out and find the cows. She supposed they'd have two groups of three and one of two.

With a sigh, she realized she was fighting a headache. Being in charge was going to be difficult. She had relied on Wes for everything, and she didn't think she could rely on Jason that way. Not that he wasn't knowledgeable. He was, but he wanted the ranch. What if he didn't help her find enough cows?

Now they had to find the cows that had gotten away during the storm last night.

She was helping Cookie make the sandwiches and store the food so it wouldn't spoil. When that was finished, Cookie made some soup for lunch, along with some sandwiches for the men. It was one o'clock before he summoned the men to lunch. Even those who had gotten up at three o'clock and who had come in and taken naps got up for lunch.

After everyone was sitting around the

campfire, Jason stood. "I have to tell you that Wes broke his ankle last night. We found him, got him in the SUV and warmed him up, but he may have to have surgery. Rosie and I are going to handle everything until we get back to the ranch. And we hope you'll do what you can to help us."

There were some murmurs running through the group of men. Jason let them talk among themselves for a few minutes. Then he said, "Wes wants to ride back to the ranch rather than take the helicopter. Rafe, I'd like you to go with Wes…and Ted. He's going back because we think he pushed Wes off his horse, which caused him to break his ankle."

More mutterings, this time louder and more heated. Jason held up a hand. "I know. I'm going to see about charging him with assault when I get back to town. But I want to be sure he's not around for now. Rafe, if you'll keep your rifle handy and wing him if he tries to get away, I think that'll do. I've got a few more instructions for you. I'll give them to you later."

Rafe nodded.

"I'll need some guards for Ted until they leave early in the morning. If there are any volunteers, please let me know. Nick has been taking care of things so far, but I think he's getting a little tired of it."

Several men said they'd take guard duty.

Then one of the men called out, "How's Rosie about all these changes?"

Rosie stepped forward. "Jason and I are going to work together to deal with everything. If you have questions or suggestions, we need to hear them. After all, some of you have a lot more experience than either of us."

The men seemed satisfied with her short speech. Jason smiled at her. She wanted to back away from him, but she knew how fragile their agreement was. She would need to present a front of complete agreement, even if she argued with Jason behind the scenes.

"Okay," Jason said. "We need someone to volunteer to relieve the men tending the herd. And two men to get some sleep because they'll be guarding Ted tonight. And someone to relieve Nick right now. Anyone else can have the rest of the day off. Tomorrow we'll hit it hard. We've got to find the lost cattle again."

Though Rosie stood beside him, smiling at the men, inside she fumed. Jason should have discussed it all with her before he announced it to the men. After all, it was still her ranch. And she intended to let him know that.

After everyone ate their lunch and went about their business, she approached him. "Can we talk?" she said sweetly.

He gave her a sharp look. "Of course. Shoot."

Don't tempt me, she thought but didn't say. Instead she invited him behind the truck, the most sheltered spot in camp. When she turned around, sweetness no longer dripped from her mouth. Now acid burned through her words as she asked, "What gave you the right to make an announcement to my employees?"

"You didn't like it? Is there something you want to change?"

"I didn't say that. But *if* there was something I wanted to change, it would be too late to change it now! We have to present a solid front if this is going to work."

"That's true. I apologize. I thought that was the best way to set things up, but I'll try to consult you before I make any announcements in the future. Will that make things better?"

She hadn't expected Jason to agree with her. She thought for sure he'd balk at her admonition. Now she was almost speechless. "I—I suppose."

To her surprise, he slipped an arm around her waist. "Honey, I promise I'll do my best, just like I promised Wes."

"I know you will, but I think I should be part of the decision-making. That's all I'm saying."

"You're absolutely right," he said, and bent down and kissed her.

Then he promptly walked away, leaving Rosie to stare after him.

This time when he'd kissed her, she hadn't jerked away. She'd been too tempted to throw her arms around his neck and give herself into the kiss. His lips were solid and firm, and for the first time since leaving the Bar G she felt warm inside.

But that couldn't happen, she reminded herself. And if Jason Barton was too much of a temptation, she'd just have to get stronger... or avoid the man altogether.

She groaned when she realized bedtime was approaching...and Wes wouldn't be in his sleeping bag.

There would be nothing between her and Jason.

When Cookie got up to fix breakfast for the three departing men, Rosemary shoved back her sleeping bag and pulled on her coat and boots. The rest of the camp appeared to still be asleep, so she didn't wake up Jason to ensure no one followed her. She felt awkward doing that anyway. Just as awkward as she'd felt sleeping near him last night. But at least he hadn't encroached on her space.

When she got back to camp, Jason was at the fire, adding some wood. She leaned down and asked Cookie how many eggs she should break and he softly said, "A dozen."

She was surprised at the amount, but she did as Cookie asked. He was ready when she passed him the bowl of beaten eggs. "Shall I go wake up Wes?" she asked.

"Jason has gone to do that." As if seeing her objection before she said it, he added, "He can help him get dressed."

"Of course," Rosemary said. "What about the other two?"

"They're both up. Jason took care of that on the way to rousing Wes."

Just as Wes, with Jason's help, reached the fire, Rosie grabbed a second canvas stool and slid it beneath Wes's broken ankle. Then she filled a plate full of food for him. "I'll get your coffee now."

"Thanks, Rosie." Wes gave her a smile that lifted her spirits more than anything had since he'd been hurt.

"No problem," she whispered, returning his smile.

Jason had sat Ted down near the fire and apparently told him not to move. Then he took his food to him. One of the other cowboys offered to guard him, apparently, and sat down next to Ted. Rosemary knew the cowboys were willing because of their loyalty and love for Wes. Rafe had gotten his breakfast and come to sit down beside Wes and they were talking quietly.

Jason handed Rosemary a plate. "Cookie said we should go ahead and eat now."

She frowned and looked at her watch. "But it's just now five o'clock."

"I know, but he made enough for us now, as well as himself."

"All right." Rosemary took the plate and filled it before sitting down on the other side of Wes.

"How are you feeling this morning, Wes?" she asked softly.

"Fine, honey, I'm fine."

"Do you hurt anywhere other than your ankle?"

"No, Rosie, I don't. You can quit worrying about me."

"She's a woman," Jason said as he sat next to Rosie. "She can't help but worry."

Rosemary whirled around to glare at him. "I don't think it's just women who worry!"

"Nope, but they do it best," Jason said, as if stating a fact.

"Don't let him upset you, Rosie," Wes said quietly.

"I won't. Don't worry about us, either, Wes. We'll be fine."

"I know you will, Rosie. You and Jason will be just fine."

By the time they'd finished, most of the men were up. They gathered around to help Wes get into the saddle. He carefully wrapped his leg around the pommel, resting his splint on the saddle. "Hey, this isn't so bad," Wes said.

"I hope you feel the same at five this afternoon," Rosie couldn't help saying.

"I'll do fine."

Rosemary bit her bottom lip and didn't say anything else. Jason reminded Rafe to keep Ted in front of the two of them. Cookie packed the food in two saddlebags, one on Wes's horse and one on Rafe's. They didn't put any on Ted's horse.

"Okay, time for us to get started," Wes said. "I'm counting on all of you, okay? I'll see you in a couple of weeks." Then he waved and turned his horse toward home.

Rosemary had never felt so alone in her life.

CHAPTER SIX

"OKAY, let's get organized," Jason called out, startling Rosemary.

She whirled around. "What are you doing?"

"Trying to not waste time, honey," Jason said, loud enough for everyone else to hear him. Then, before she could realize what he was doing, he wrapped his arms around her and whispered, "Remember, we must present a united front."

She stiffened and nodded. Then she pulled away and walked back to the fire. "Cookie, is there anything we can do to help?"

"Naw, I've got it all under control. Grab a cup and have some coffee."

Jason filled two cups, gave one to Rosemary and guided her to two empty canvas stools. "Go ahead and eat," he told the cowboys. "We ate with Wes before he left."

"Do you think he's going to make it all

right?" Nick asked. "That looked mighty un-comfortable."

"I couldn't agree more," Jason said with a laugh, "but I have absolute faith that Wes will get there fine."

Rosemary spoke up. "I intend to call Sara Beth a little later and tell her to put a mattress in the back of the truck and go meet him. He should be willing to ride in the truck by then."

"I bet he'll be glad to see her," one of the other cowboys said with a chuckle.

"Yeah, that's a good idea, honey," Jason said, flashing her a smile. "Now we've lost four riders, which brings us to ten total. Do you think two of you can still keep the herd from getting away?"

"Since we lost some of the cattle, yeah, but if we get up to seventy-five head, we can't." Nick looked at the cowboys around him for agreement and they were nodding their heads.

"Okay, that leaves eight of us to search for cows. We'll do two groups of three and one of two, I guess, unless you think two of you can do an effective job?"

The men around the fire straightened up, as if Jason had challenged them. "We can do it with just two of us!" one of them said.

"No. I don't want to risk that until we have to," Rosemary said. "While we're in rough country, let's do two groups of three and you and I will be the group of two."

Jason nodded. "Okay, honey, we'll do it your way."

His constant use of endearments did strange things to her stomach but she concentrated instead on what Jason was doing to organize the cowboys. "Of course, we'll have to cover more territory." She gave the parameters of each area and checked with the two groups of cowboys. "Is everyone okay with that?"

They all nodded.

"Then we'll head out when we've finished breakfast. In the meantime, Jason and I will go relieve the two guys on the herd."

Jason followed her from the fire and they saddled their horses side by side.

"You did a good job this morning, Rosie," Jason said softly.

"I thought we did a good job...together."

He was right about presenting a united front, but Rosie had to be honest. Now that the cowboys weren't around, she realized her skin still tingled from Jason's touch. How was she going to keep up the pretense for the rest of the roundup?

They worked hard that day, covering a lot of territory and driving the cattle they found back to camp. Much to Rosemary's surprise, she and Jason worked well together. She came to a halt and pulled out her cell phone after a couple of hours.

"Sara Beth, it's Rosie."

"What's wrong?"

"I wish nothing was, but your feelings were right. Wes got hurt. It's a broken ankle. Cookie says he may need surgery."

"Oh, my, when will the helicopter get here?"

"That's just it. He refused the helicopter." She told Sara Beth how her husband, stubborn and determined as he was, was making his way home. "I thought you might put a mattress in the truck and drive out to meet them."

"Good idea. I'll do that at once and call the hospital to let them know we're coming."

"Good. Sara Beth, I—I'm sorry he got hurt. The man who shoved him off his horse—"

"What? Who did such a thing? I'll kill him!"

"No, you won't. We don't want you to go to jail. Tell Rafe to take the man to the sheriff."

"Who is it?"

"Jason's manager, or he was supposed to be."

"Why did the man— Did he do the same thing to Jesse?"

"We think so, but we don't have evidence to prove that. How is Jesse?"

"He got out of the hospital yesterday. He wanted to ride back out to join you again, but I told him no."

"I'm glad. He can ride out with you now and help with Wes. He might be cranky after riding that long in the saddle."

"I'll be glad to see him no matter what."

"I know. Take good care of him."

"I will, but you be careful. Is Jason behaving himself?"

Did she consider a few hugs and kisses misbehaving? But they were only pretend, she reminded herself.

"Yes. He's fine." She cleared her throat and focused on the roundup. "We're already recouping the cows we lost because of the storm. I'll call again in a couple of days. Hopefully with good news that I saved the ranch."

* * *

When they were all once again around the campfire that night, there was no conversation. Everyone was exhausted. But they had found almost all the cattle, and the herd was now even larger.

Three men were needed to circle the herd, leaving them with two groups of two and one group of three. It was going to take them longer since they were each searching a wider area. Rosemary was feeling discouraged. She stared at her plate of food, not eating.

"Rosie, did you lose your appetite?" Jason whispered.

She jerked her head up to notice everyone staring at her. "No, I'm just a little tired. I'm not as strong as you men!" she said, trying to laugh.

She thought she failed miserably, but it seemed to satisfy the men.

Jason whispered, "Try to eat some more. They'll all be checking your plate."

She knew he was right, but she hated admitting it. She struggled with her dinner. When she'd finished more than half, she stood and left the fire. Cookie had a scrap bucket that he emptied out each morning before he moved camp, and she dumped the rest of her food in there, hoping no one noticed. Then she washed her plate.

"Don't any of you cowboys sing? I understood they always have a singing cowboy on these roundups," Jason said.

"Hey, Nick sings," one of the cowboys said. "He even brought his guitar. I saw it in Cookie's SUV."

Jason looked at Nick. "I think tonight would be a good time for some singing. Raise the spirit around here," he said, glancing in Rosemary's direction.

"I don't feel—" Nick began, but one of the cowboys next to him dug an elbow in his ribs. "Oh! Oh, yeah, we can all sing. Rosie, you come join us, okay?"

She was standing beside the SUV, as if she didn't know where to go. Jason got up and put his arm around her. "Sure, she'll come join us. I bet she has a great singing voice."

He bent down and whispered in her ear, "Come on, help us keep everyone cheerful."

She returned to the fire while Nick went to get his guitar. Jason kept his arm around her even though she tried to shrug it off.

He leaned over and whispered, "We have to convince them everything's all right."

She drew a deep breath and smiled at Cookie. "That was a good meal tonight, Cookie. If I ever think about getting married, I'm going to have to get you to teach me to cook."

"Anytime, Rosie."

Nick began strumming on his guitar. "What do you want to sing first, Rosie? How about an old one? We'll do 'Home on the Range.'"

The notes of the guitar drifted in the night air and several of the men joined Nick in singing the old song. Soon they were all singing around the fire.

Rosemary was the last to join in. She found herself listening to the clear baritone of Jason's voice. It, too, demonstrated his strength, his enthusiasm. He didn't try to dominate the singing, even though his voice was good enough.

After he squeezed her shoulder, she joined in. Their communication amazed her. She wasn't sure how she knew what he wanted, but she seemed able to anticipate whatever he wanted from her. Probably because what he wanted was what she should do in the first place.

About five songs later, Nick did a solo of a

popular song she liked, "I Cross My Heart." It was a very romantic song, and Jason pulled her just a little closer to him. She couldn't keep from looking up at him, wondering what he was thinking.

Probably that it would be good for the men to think they had a thing for each other.

Of course, she wouldn't agree with him, but by his actions alone, she realized he'd created the aura that doing what he said was doing what she wanted. And she couldn't argue with him. The most important thing was the roundup. And it would be best served if they were led by one voice, whether it came from Jason or from her.

"I think I need to call it a night, guys," Rosemary finally said, standing. "It's been a long day. But you've all been great. If we just hang together for a little longer, we'll be back home again, with Jesse and Wes. Thank you."

Amid all the good-nights, Jason said good-night also and followed her from the firelight. She'd left her bedroll by the SUV and she recognized Jason's right beside hers.

"Go ahead. I'll keep guard," Jason said, mimicking Wes's quiet words each night.

Trying to hide sudden tears, Rosemary

excused herself. When she returned a few minutes later, Jason was sitting on his bedroll.

"Everything all right?" he asked.

She nodded and rolled back the top of her bedroll. Removing her boots, she stored them in the bottom of her bedroll. Then she removed her coat and folded it on top of her saddle to serve as her pillow. "Good night."

Before she realized it, Jason leaned forward and kissed her lips again. "Good night."

She lay silently while he settled in his sleeping bag about two inches from hers. Finally she said, "Jason, I think you're overdoing it."

"Overdoing what?" he asked softly, turning to face her.

"The k-kissing and stuff. You've made your point, and I'll admit it's a good thing, but don't push it."

He leaned even closer. "Honey, I'm holding back the best I can because I promised Wes I would. But once this roundup is over, I'll be freed from that promise. Then you'd better watch out."

Though her heart rate took off, she kept her voice steady. "Don't make promises you don't intend to keep, Mr. Barton."

His eyes widened and a slow grin grew on his face. "That's more encouragement than you've ever given me, Ms. Wilson. I won't forget."

He kissed her again and then lay back and closed his eyes.

Rosie lay there, pulse pounding, lips on fire. She'd intended for her words to slow him down. Instead he'd taken it as encouragement.

Dear Lord, she prayed, what did I just do?

Jason knew at once the next morning that he'd revealed too much last night. Rosie was distant now, holding herself stiff whenever he came close. She deliberately chose a camp stool between two of the men at breakfast, not leaving him a chance to sit beside her.

One of the cowboys immediately offered to give up his seat to Jason, but Rosie quietly told him it wasn't necessary. Jason watched concern race around the campfire. He needed to do something to keep things settled. He leaned toward the next man and said, "I think I'm rushing Rosie, but she's so damn sweet. I'm going to have to back off a little until we get this roundup finished."

He knew it wouldn't take long before his

comments were passed on. Cowboys gossiped as much as any other group, especially when the gossip was about someone they cared about. And, to a man, they all cared about Rosie.

When he made the assignments that morning, he told Rosie he thought she should stay behind to work the herd rather than search for more stray cattle. He knew that would make for an easier day. Her surprise meant she'd be coming to speak to him personally, for the first time since last night.

But his reasoning was that riding the herd was the only job she could do without him. No way was he sending her out with another man to work all day.

"Why do you think you can assign me to working the herd?" she demanded in a whisper as the cowboys left the campfire.

"I thought you could have an easier day for a change. You can ride out tomorrow. Besides, it's not fair for Robert to work the herd every day. He was beginning to think we thought he was too old to do his job."

Uncertainty filled her eyes as she considered his words. "Are you sure?"

"Didn't you see his reaction when I said he could ride out?"

"No, I was too upset that I—Was he pleased?"

"Yeah. A big grin broke on his face. He was the first to saddle his horse."

"All right, just for today. You promise?"

"You bet." He started to add a kiss, but she quickly moved away before he could.

Rosemary relieved one of the cowboys who'd been caring for the herd since 2:00 a.m. that morning. She knew he was expected to ride out after eating his breakfast. Being a cowboy might look glamorous to some people, but Rosemary knew once you'd done the job, you realized the strength and stamina it took.

She and the two other cowboys assigned to the herd for the day circled the cows they'd found. Rosie spent her time trying to estimate the number of cows they now had collected. Her best guess was a hundred and fifty head. Which meant they weren't that far from their goal.

Of course, even if they had two hundred head of cattle at the end of the day, they still had a lot of land to cover, but they expected to find most of the missing cattle in the rough hills.

If they found more cattle in the flatter land,

that would give them some operating funds for the winter. Rosemary hadn't wanted to think about the winter. There was less work in the winter, but the costs skyrocketed when the weather got bad. She'd need to buy some hay as their own crop wasn't enough to make it through the snowy months.

Doing the monotonous work of riding around the herd, Rosemary had time for a niggling worry to build into a massive fear. Would she retain the ranch only to lose it when she couldn't keep it going? Even thinking about that caused her stomach to twist. She couldn't let that happen. But the weight of everyone who depended on her made it even more difficult.

Would she even be able to sleep at night, worrying about handling all the duties and costs of running a ranch?

And was that really what she wanted, or what she thought her parents wanted for her? No, she knew she wanted to be a rancher, to live on the land and find a way to make ends meet.

But it was going to be a challenge. The biggest of her life.

* * *

Jason rode out that morning with Nick.

"You and Rosie having problems?" Nick asked as soon as they were away from camp.

"Not problems, exactly. But I realized I was pressing her too hard, what with all she's dealing with. I can bide my time until we get back home. Mind you, I'm not giving up my stake, so don't plan on taking over." He grinned at Nick, letting him know he knew how the cowboy felt about Rosie.

Nick nodded. "I know that. I just wanted to make sure that Rosie was okay."

"Oh, yeah, she's as fine as they come."

Both men grinned in agreement. Then they got down to the job at hand. For the first time, they were riding ahead of camp. Cookie hadn't moved his camp the past couple of days. Now they rode ahead and would drive the cattle they found back to the main herd. Which meant he'd have a chance to check on Rosie.

He missed riding with her, but he could only blame himself. He believed she'd had such a hard day yesterday that she needed a more relaxing one today. He knew he couldn't keep her in camp, helping Cookie. There was no way she'd agree to that.

He let his mind drift as he pictured Rosie in

her element, chasing cows, her face alive with excitement. Just looking at her raised his own excitement level…but it wasn't about cows. He found the woman attractive. And sexy. But with a woman like Rosie and under circumstances like these, he had to take it slow.

Hence, here he was sharing his day with Nick instead of Rosie. It wasn't the same.

About that time he heard his name being called faintly. He looked around and saw Nick slumped over his saddle. With foreboding, Jason rushed his horse to Nick's side.

"What's wrong?"

"I—I just threw up. I don't know what—" He broke off as he became sick again.

Jason tried to brace Nick without getting in his way. When Nick was sitting up straight again, he asked, "Was it something you ate? Or a stomach virus?"

"I don't know, but I started feeling bad about half an hour ago."

"Okay, we'd better get you back to camp." Damn, if Nick went down they'd only have six looking for cows. And if it was a virus, it might put the entire roundup on hold.

They made their way slowly back to camp, with pauses for Nick to retch again. He was exhausted and barely able to stay in the saddle.

Jason was really becoming alarmed at the extent of Nick's illness.

When they reached camp, he hollered for Cookie, who appeared at once. Jason told him what happened.

Cookie caught Nick as he fell out of the saddle. "What's making him sick?"

"I don't know. I'm hoping it's not a virus that'll run all the way through the group." Jason got off his horse, letting the reins trail the ground while he took Nick's horse to the rope corral.

When he returned to the campfire, he found Cookie settling Nick in his bedroll close to the fire.

"He's got the shivers right now, and burning up with fever. I've given him some stomach medicine and some Ibuprofen for his fever.

About that time, they heard more horses. Jason looked up to see Rosie riding toward him with the cowboy beside her slumped over his horse.

"Uh-oh. Looks like Nick is just the beginning." He moved forward to assist Rosemary.

Cookie, who'd been about to put the medicine away, changed his mind. He followed Jason to meet Rosie and her sick partner.

The two men got the rider off his horse and to the campfire. Cookie assessed the situation while Jason turned to Rosie.

"How are you feeling?"

"Fine. Why?"

"This is our second patient today. Nick came down with the same symptoms, only we were a little farther away."

"Oh, no! If something runs through everyone, we'll come to a complete halt."

"I'm afraid so. We can only pray it's a twenty-four-hour bug and not longer."

"Oh, no!"

"Don't panic, Rosie. Right now it's only two men. As soon as I make sure Cookie's got everything under control, I'll come help with the herd."

She clenched her teeth and nodded before she swung her horse back toward the herd.

Jason turned to ask Cookie if he had everything under control when he heard other horses coming toward them. Not a good sign.

CHAPTER SEVEN

ROSEMARY'S concern was interrupted by her phone ringing. She hurriedly answered it.

"Hello?"

"Hi, honey, it's Sara Beth."

"How's Wes? Did you get him to the hospital?"

"Yes, he's there, but they're postponing the surgery a day or two."

"Was his ankle too swollen?"

"No, not too bad. Uh, how are things there?"

Rosemary considered her answer, but she decided to lie. There was no need to worry Sara Beth. "Fine. Everyone will be glad to hear Wes is okay. Did Jesse help Rafe get Ted to the sheriff's office?"

"Yes, they took him there. But the sheriff said he could only hold him for forty-eight hours. They argued with him, but he didn't promise anything."

"Oh. Maybe I won't tell the men about that."

"You're sure everything is okay?

"Why do you ask, Sara Beth?"

"Well, I'd better tell you so you'll be prepared. You see, the weekend before y'all started the cattle drive, I was at a church committee meeting and—and they were talking about a twenty-four-hour virus going around. I didn't think anything about it, but two days ago, I was sick as a dog. I couldn't stop throwing up. That's why they can't operate on Wes. He's got the virus, too. And then Rafe and Jesse got sick, too. I'm afraid I've infected the entire bunch of cowboys."

Rosemary sighed. "So far it's only two of the men who are sick, but it sounds like the rest of us may have it, too. You said it only lasted twenty-four hours?"

"Yes, honey, I'm so sorry. Do you want Rafe and Jesse to ride back out?"

"No, they might get sick all over again. We'll manage. It just may take us a little bit longer. Don't worry."

"You don't try to do everything by yourself, now. You hear me? Let others share the load."

"I will. Everyone always pitches in, Sara Beth, I promise." Before she hung up she added, "Give Wes my love and take good care of him. Will you call me after he comes out of surgery?"

"I will."

Then she ended the call before Sara Beth could hear her cry. It didn't stop Rosemary from crying. She wished she could head home today, away from the problems. But if she did, she'd be giving up the ranch.

And she couldn't do that.

"Rosie?"

Rosemary pulled her horse to a stop and hurriedly wiped her cheeks. She recognized Jason's voice and braced herself for more bad news.

"Are you okay?"

"Yes. Sara Beth called. She thinks she gave everyone the virus. She had it, then Wes, Rafe and Jesse."

"How long does it last?" Jason asked, frowning.

"Twenty-four hours."

"Well, that's a relief. Kenneth just rode in sick, too. His partner is going to join the group still out working. We're down to seven people plus Cookie. With three of us on the herd, it leaves four people to search for cows." He rubbed the back of his neck, which shoved his hat forward on his head, shading his eyes. "It's going to slow things down, honey."

"Do you think I'm an idiot? I know that!"

"Sorry. I know you do. I'm just trying to figure out what to do."

"I think we put two people on the herd and start pushing them forward, as long as Cookie can move the camp. If we have too many sick, we'll just have to take a day off and hope most of them recover quickly."

"Good thinking." They rode along in silence for a moment. Then he said, "Don't worry about the deadline. These are extraordinary times. I'll give you more time."

"I haven't given up!" she exclaimed. "And I'm not asking for any concessions. We still have a couple of weeks. All I'm asking is that you help us. So go do your job!"

He rode off without a word, moving around the cattle ahead of her.

Rosemary felt ashamed of herself. She'd need to apologize to him. He'd been trying to make it easier for her, but she'd treated his offer like a slap in the face.

Wes would be ashamed of her, too. That alone told her she had to apologize to Jason.

But she could wait until they reached camp, assuming there was someone to relieve them.

About four, two riders brought a dozen head of cattle to join the herd. Then they sought out Rosemary to tell her the other two were in camp, sick. What did she want them to do?

"I want you to go into camp, relax, have dinner. If you're still okay, come back and relieve a couple of us to get dinner. Then I'll come back and relieve the third person."

"But we could let you go in and rest now, Rosie. I mean, you're a great cowboy, but you might be too tired."

About that time, Jason rode up to join in the conversation. He agreed that Rosie should go in now and eat and relax.

"Please! I'm not in need of a manicure or a massage. I can herd the cows for a few more hours. Just do what I said."

"And if you come down with the flu, see if someone can come tell us."

The two cowboys headed for the camp and Jason prepared to ride back to his position.

"Jason?" Rosemary called out.

"Yeah?"

"I wanted to apologize for my reaction to

your generosity. That was very rude of me and I want to say I'm sorry."

After a pause, he said, "Okay, thanks," and rode away.

Rosemary didn't think he believed she was sorry. But she was. She owed him a lot. Managing the roundup without Wes would've been much more difficult without Jason. He was good with the men and seemed to understand them better than her. She wouldn't have kept a stiff upper lip last night without his insistence.

With a sigh, she turned back to her job. It might not be exciting, but it certainly was important. She didn't want to have to find these cows all over again.

It was dark before anyone rode out to the herd. The two cowboys who'd talked to her earlier reappeared to relieve two of the three herding the cows.

"Go relieve Jason and Larry. I'm good for now."

"Rosie, you need to eat," one of the men insisted.

"Then ride back to camp and ask Cookie for a sandwich or something I can eat in the saddle. Then I'll stay here until the shift change at two."

"I'm not sure there'll be a shift change. We're the only two not sick at camp. So, at two, we'll be able to manage the herd by ourselves. You just go on in then, okay?"

"Okay. But will you be able to work all night?"

"Yeah, the cows will be asleep. It'll be easy."

"I'll be back with something for you to eat in a few minutes," the other cowboy promised and turned back toward camp.

The first cowboy rode ahead and tried to relieve Jason. Rosemary could see the discussion the two had. Then Jason rode back to talk to her.

"What the hell do you think you're doing?" he demanded, anger in his voice.

"I'm riding herd. What do you think I'm doing?" She was in no mood to placate the man.

"They're all worried about you. Go back to camp so you can reassure them."

"Jason, this is my responsibility. It's what Wes would do if he were here. So it's what I'm doing."

"Wes is a man. You're—"

"A woman. Do you really want to have this argument?"

"Rosie, you're not thinking straight. I know you're a strong person, but you are a little weaker than a man. Even you have to admit that."

"I'm not doing something that requires great strength. All I have to do is stay in the saddle. One of the guys is bringing me dinner. I'll be fine."

"So you think I should go sit by the fire and enjoy my food while you ride herd? I don't think so!"

She drew a deep breath. "Okay, send them back to the camp to get some rest. The two of us can manage the herd. They can get a good night's rest and relieve us at six in the morning. That way we can maintain the herd. We won't try to move the herd or camp until more people are available."

With a gusty sigh, Jason said, "Okay, I'll go tell the other guy and send him for my dinner and tell him to reassure the camp about you."

Rosemary knew Jason was frustrated with her, but she had to do her job. Maybe if they could maintain their position for twenty-four hours—no, make that thirty-six hours—they'd have enough men to manage.

* * *

Early the next morning, as the sky in the east began to grow lighter, Rosemary heard the sound of three cowboys coming to relieve her and Jason. She'd dozed a little during the night, but she was definitely ready for her bedroll. After a good breakfast.

"Rosie," Jerry, one of the cowboys, said as he reached her.

She braced herself. She knew what the tone of voice meant. Trouble.

"What is it?"

"Cookie's sick."

Rosemary's heart sank. Cookie was such an important part of the roundup. She'd heard someone say a soldier marched on his stomach. Well, cowboys worked on their stomachs. Without good meals, production would go down. And she knew who had to replace Cookie.

"All right, Jerry. I'll take over for a day. Then Cookie will be back on his feet."

"But you'll need some sleep, Rosie. You haven't slept all night."

"I dozed some. Maggie is well-trained, you know. It won't be too bad, and when we get back to the ranch, I'll sleep for a week." She managed a reassuring smile. "Thanks for coming out to relieve me. I'll try to send someone out for you."

"Thanks, Rosie. You're the best!"

She turned Maggie toward camp. She'd seen the other two cowboys join Jerry, which meant Jason would be coming to camp, also. She'd try to make him go to sleep without mentioning Cookie being sick.

Someone had to keep going.

She found Cookie still trying to cook breakfast for them when she reached the camp. She took over at once and had Nick, who was almost over the virus, help Cookie to bed and give him the medicine he'd been distributing to everyone.

When Jason reached the camp, she had breakfast ready for him. Everyone else had eaten if they could keep it down.

"You ready to get some sleep, Rosie?" Jason asked as he finished his breakfast.

"Yes, I'll be right there. I just need to check with Cookie. You go on to sleep."

She did feel a little more energetic after eating. She washed her dishes and then went to the truck where Cookie slept. He was stretched out in the back seat, moaning.

"Cookie, is there anything I can get you?" she asked.

"No, just let me be."

"Okay, I'll check on you in a little bit."

"Rosie, I'm sorry!"

"Not to worry. It's not your fault."

Then she went around the campfire, checking on all the men who were sick. Fortunately there wasn't a lot to do. The virus had to run its course, and no one felt like eating.

She checked on Jason and found him asleep. No doubt he'd given in to fatigue while waiting for her. She covered him, letting her fingers linger along his jaw as she tucked in the cover. He was a downright gorgeous man, and she surrendered to the urge to study him in the early morning sun.

After feasting her full, she got into her bedroll and stretched out, this time turning to face him. For as long as she was awake, she'd have him to look at.

Jason had been determined that he would not succumb to the flu, but when he awakened from a deep sleep, his stomach in distress, he knew he'd failed in that respect.

Throwing back his bedroll, he managed to stumble a few feet from the camp before he got sick. Suddenly arms came around him to brace him, one hand going to his forehead. Since his legs were weak, he welcomed the support.

"It's okay," Rosemary said softly. "I'll help you back to your bedroll and get the medicine. You're running a fever."

"I'm sorry, Rosie. I didn't think I'd get sick." His voice sounded like an old man's voice, startling him.

"Don't worry, Jason. It's not your fault. Would you like some beef broth?" She'd made it after she'd napped. "It might give you a little strength."

"No!" he said vehemently, though his voice wasn't loud. He couldn't bear the thought of putting anything in his stomach.

She helped him back to his bedroll and put hers over him for additional warmth.

"I—I can't g-go ride herd," he muttered as he closed his eyes.

"No, of course not," a sweet voice said, patting his shoulder.

And that was the last thing he remembered.

Rosemary stared down at him. He'd tried to help her all he could. She couldn't resist bending down and kissing his forehead. He'd never know, and she wanted the contact with him. But now she'd be on her own.

Nick and Ken were finally recovering a little. She gave them each a cup of broth to test their stomachs.

"This tastes good, Rosie," Nick managed to say.

Rosemary grinned. "I'm glad. If you can keep it down, I'll do a better job of cooking for supper."

"I hope I can. I don't want to go through that again."

Ken was a little more reluctant to test his stomach, but she assured him he was on the mend and needed the soup to give him some strength.

Though she made periodic rounds to the sick, Rosemary noticed she visited Jason more than the others. She told herself it was because her life was easier if he was strong. But she was afraid she was growing too fond of him. Unlike last night when she merely gazed at him, today she let herself touch him. She stroked his forehead gently, let her hand travel over the stubble on his jaw.

She could no longer deny it. She was attracted to Jason. What she felt was no pretense. It was the real thing. A man-woman thing.

An attraction she could never act on.

There wouldn't be a happy ending, she realized. If she kept the ranch, Jason would go away. If he won the ranch, she would go away. No matter what happened, they only had the roundup.

Tearing herself away, she checked on the other men and the herd. She had a feeling the three riders might turn up sick before dark.

Around noon, she made some sandwiches and got Nick to take them to the guys tending the herd. He didn't come back alone.

Jerry had fallen ill. Rosemary helped get him off his horse, put him in his bedroll near the fire and gave him medicine.

His sandwich was untouched, so she ate it herself. She needed to keep her strength up.

As any of the cowboys woke up without fever, she encouraged them to eat the soup, along with some vanilla pudding she'd made. For the healthy crew she made a chicken casserole and hot biscuits. She served it to the couple of cowboys who'd reached the stage of wanting something to eat. Then she asked Nick and Ken to go ride herd for a little while.

Their spirits were willing, but she wasn't sure about their bodies. But, as she'd expected, the two who'd been riding herd all day were doubled over their saddles when they reached camp. As they apologized for causing any trouble, she helped them down. It took all of Rosemary's strength to get them to their bedrolls. One of the cowboys who was feeling better tended to their horses.

Giving them the medicine wasn't as difficult. This virus brought even hardened cowboys to their knees very quickly.

She surveyed the camp. Finally everyone seemed settled, including Jason, who was sleeping soundly. She longed to climb into her bedroll and shut her eyes, too, but she had to keep the fire going. It was cold and the fever left the men shivering even in their bedrolls.

As the evening passed, she dozed by the fire. When she suddenly came awake, she checked her watch to see it was nearing two o'clock. After checking everyone and finding no one awake, she saddled her horse and rode out to the herd.

She sent Nick and Ken to their beds, asking them to send someone else out in the morning so she could come fix breakfast and tend to the sick ones. She wasn't sure they would remember her request, though; they were exhausted.

As was she. But someone had to keep the herd in place. Fortunately most of the cows were asleep. As long as nothing came along to disturb them, like coyotes or wolves or a thunderstorm, she'd be okay. She hoped.

Jason woke up the next morning with a sense of urgency. He quickly noticed his stomach seemed stable; in fact, he was starving. A quick look told him no one else was stirring. He checked the time and realized it was almost seven.

He shoved back his bedroll and found he'd been covered by Rosie's bedroll, too. Where was she?

His legs were wobbly, which surprised him. He managed to get to the campfire and discovered the fire almost out. However, there was a pot of broth on the fire. He threw on some wood, enough to get the fire going again. Then he poured some of the liquid in a cup.

As he drank his cupful, several others around the camp woke up. Jason recommended they try the soup, but he was more intent on finding Rosie.

He remembered Rosie's voice telling him to go to sleep. But nothing more. Somehow he managed to get his horse saddled, though he was amazed at how weak he was. As he finished, Nick appeared beside him.

"Rosie relieved us at the herd at about 2:00 a.m., I think. I don't remember much. I was so tired. But I can go ride herd now. I'm better."

"Did you get any breakfast? If not, stay and eat something. The soup, at least," he added, when Nick didn't look too enthused. "Or try to make something everyone can eat. And add some wood to the fire. Then come to the herd, with someone else if possible. I'm going out to be sure she's okay."

"All right, Jason. I'll be out as quick as I can."

Jason was glad Nick turned away before Jason tried to mount his horse. He had a feeling it wouldn't be too graceful. He counted it as a big accomplishment when he managed to get upright in the saddle.

When he reached the herd, he saw Rosie on the far side, moving slowly. She must be completely exhausted, because as he watched, she bent over her saddle. Or was she sick?

He rode around the herd as quickly as he

could. "Are you all right, honey?" he demanded roughly.

"I'm fine. Go back to camp."

Her voice was dull and her eyes glazed with fever. He reached out to touch her cheek, but she jerked away.

Gently he said, "I think you have fever, Rosie."

"Yeah."

"That means you're sick," he said, afraid she didn't realize it.

"Yeah."

"Rosie, you need to go get in your bedroll and take some medicine."

"I have to take care of the herd. It's my job."

"The herd's not going anywhere. Come on. Some of the guys will be out here as soon as they've had breakfast."

"I forgot. I have to cook breakfast."

Jason was becoming very concerned about her dazed state, but if she thought she had to cook breakfast, that would at least get her moving toward camp.

"Okay, honey, let's go fix breakfast."

He took her reins, not sure she had any idea where camp was. Once he got her there, he could help her, he hoped, as she'd helped him.

The men met them as they reached the campfire, all of them realizing Rosemary wasn't in good shape.

Jason sprang down from his horse to catch Rosie as she slid out of her saddle. He managed to carry her to the SUV, though his legs were shaking. Nick went ahead of him and opened the door to the back seat.

"Is she okay?" Nick asked.

"I don't know. Where's Cookie?"

"He's coming."

Cookie got in the front seat on his knees so he could see Rosemary in the back. He took her pulse and fever, frowning.

"She's been sick most of the night, I think," Jason said, "but she kept riding around the herd all by herself."

"I'll get the medicine. Let's leave her here in the truck. I'll keep checking on her. How about you? Are you recovered?"

"Yeah. Well, almost. I can ride." Jason wasn't going to moan and sit around the fire when Rosie had stayed in the saddle all night long, sick.

"Come eat some breakfast first. Serve yourself while I get medicine for Rosie." Cookie went to the back of the SUV to collect the stomach medicine and ibuprofen for fever.

When he came back, he found Jason still hovering over Rosie. "Come on, Jason, she's going to be all right."

"I just don't remember being this bad. Maybe it's because she refused to give in to it."

Cookie agreed. "But we might've lost most of the herd if she hadn't stayed out there."

Jason realized then what a remarkable woman Rosie was. She'd do whatever it took to earn his down payment and to hold on to the Bar G. The ranch meant that much to her.

No surprise there, since it was her heritage, her birthright.

What surprised him was how much he wanted her to have it.

CHAPTER EIGHT

WITH only Rosie down sick, they were able to form two groups of three, leaving three men on the herd. They were to slowly move the herd toward the ranch.

Cookie would keep camp where it was for today. Jason wanted him to keep a close eye on Rosie. He was worried about her.

They rode hard all day and pulled in about another sixty head of cattle. By Jason's estimate, they were over two hundred, as Rosie had predicted.

When he and his teammates reached camp, his first priority was to check on Rosie. Cookie intercepted him.

"Jason, don't wake her. I think it's the first decent sleep she's had all day."

"Why?"

"She's been sick a lot. I tried to get her to eat some of the beef broth, but she couldn't keep it down. I'm afraid she's getting dehydrated."

"Do we need to fly her to a hospital?"

"Let's give it another day. If she's not better and keeping down at least some water, we'll consider that."

"Okay. I'm just going to look at her. I won't wake her," Jason promised as he moved past Cookie.

He opened the front door and crawled in to look over the seat at Rosemary. She lay curled up under the cover, her cheeks flushed, her lashes lying on her cheeks. He wanted to touch her so badly, he actually linked his hands together, pressing hard to keep them from straying.

"How is she?" Nick whispered from behind him.

Jason jerked around. "She's sleeping. Cookie says it's her first good sleep all day." He backed out of the SUV. "Is supper ready?"

"Yeah. Everyone's feeling okay. They'll feel better after a good meal. I hope Rosie recovers as fast."

"Me, too." He was almost out of the SUV when both men heard a telephone ring.

Jason realized at once what it was. "Rosie's

cell phone." He bent back over the front seat to dig for it in her pocket. Rosie stirred but didn't wake up.

"Hello?" Jason said.

"Who is this?"

"Jason Barton."

"Where's Rosie?"

"Who is this?" Jason asked in return.

"It's Sara Beth, Wes's wife."

"Rosie is sleeping. She got the bug, like we all did, but she kept going without telling anyone until this morning."

"Is she okay?"

"Cookie thinks she'll recover soon," Jason lied. "How's Wes?"

"He's out of surgery. He'll have to get around on crutches for at least a week before they'll put a walking cast on him."

"Sounds like he's in good hands."

"Yes. I wish I had Rosie here, too."

"I understand, Sara Beth, but we'll be in probably in five or six days."

"Okay. Give Rosie our love."

"I will, as soon as she wakes up. I'll have her call you when she gets well."

"I'll be waiting."

He disconnected the call. "I don't think I should've said that."

"Why?" Nick asked, having remained beside him.

"If Rosie doesn't get well soon, Sara Beth will worry."

"Yeah, like the rest of us."

"I know." He kept Rosie's cell phone to make sure no one could call and disturb her sleep. "Let's go get a good meal. I'm starving."

He quietly closed the door and retreated to the campfire. After he ate, he would go ride herd for about six hours. Then he'd grab a few hours sleep and be up again to search the hills for stray cows. Though he wanted nothing else, he didn't have time to moon over Rosie.

Still, thoughts of her took up permanent residence in his mind. As he rode around the herd with Nick and Ken, he thought about Rosie all the time. She was stronger than any woman he'd ever known. His wife hadn't been willing to lift a finger. Not that he expected her to do all the work. He'd hired a housekeeper. But their house hadn't been that big. She'd expected breakfast in bed, after he'd gone to work. Then she'd gone to the gym each morning. Shopping was always on for the afternoon, and parties each night. When he tired of the party circuit, she'd continued without him.

He later discovered she'd done some other things without him, too, particularly with her private trainer. By that time, Jason hadn't cared. They had divorced as soon as possible, and he'd paid a lot for his freedom.

He swore it wasn't something he'd give up again.

But he was thinking about doing so now. Rosie was everything he wanted in a woman. She was her own person, and she was willing to work hard for what she wanted. The fact that she was beautiful was a plus, but not a necessity. Her warmth and love for those around her counted a lot more.

But he wouldn't know if she cared for him unless he lost the ranch to her. If he won the ranch, she might accept his proposal just to retain control of her home.

That thought worried him all evening as he circled the cattle. So he'd have to lose the ranch to gain Rosie's love? It would be worth it, wouldn't it?

* * *

When Cookie awakened him the next morning, Jason's first question was about Rosie. "How's she doing this morning?"

"I got her to keep down some water last night. This morning I'll try the beef broth."

"Can I give it to her?"

"Jason, I really think she should sleep as long as she can. I think—"

Rosie's cell phone rang. Jason dug it out of his coat pocket. "Hello?"

"Jason, it's Wes."

"How are you, Wes?"

"Never mind me. There's a big snowstorm coming. You need to start moving what you have to the ranch as fast as you can."

"Snow? Are you sure?"

"As sure as we can ever be about weather."

"But we could find more cattle if we had today."

"Listen to me, Jason. You must start home today. If a snowstorm hits up in the mountains, you could lose some of the herd. You can get close in enough by tonight that the snowfall won't be much. But as high up as you are right now, it could get bad."

Jason had enough respect for Wes to obey his orders. "Okay, Wes."

"We'll be waiting for you in the early afternoon tomorrow."

"Okay."

He got off the phone and turned back to the campfire. "That was Wes. He says there's a big snowstorm coming and we've got to head for the ranch as quickly as we can." The cowboys murmured among themselves about bad luck. Jason hurried to tell them all was not lost. "We've got over two hundred head, like Rosie thought. I'd hoped to get more for her, but Wes says we have no choice."

"How do we handle this?" Nick asked.

"Seven of us will drive the herd, and two men will bring the horses. Cookie, you'll need to break camp and drive ahead of us to the next camp. You'd better pack some dry wood if we're going to have a hot meal this evening."

"I'll start packing as soon as I clean up from breakfast and make some sandwiches."

Jason nodded. "Okay, I need two guys to go with me to relieve the three out there now. We'll start moving the herd slowly, waiting for the rest of you. And bring our sandwiches when Cookie gets them ready."

He paused by Cookie as he moved toward

the rope corral. "You'll keep an eye on Rosie, won't you?"

"You know I will."

"I'm counting on you, Cookie."

He rode out to relieve the other men, surprising them with the news. He chose two of them to bring the horses on ropes. The third one would ride drag as soon as they had breakfast.

Though it was difficult with only three of them, they began moving the herd. Half an hour later, the others joined them.

"Did you see any sign of Rosie?" Jason asked, concern in his voice.

The men exchanged glances, but they told him no.

Jason sent two cowboys up each side of the herd and he remained behind the herd with two other riders. Already the air was getting colder and storm clouds were gathering. He guessed Wes had been right about the forecast.

Within ten minutes, the snow started falling. September was early for a snowstorm, but it happened. Jason put on his slicker, and he advised all the cowboys to do the same. The bright yellow would make them all more visible in the falling snow. Driving the wild cattle was more difficult than a normal herd, but they kept them under control.

But Jason's mind was settled on Rosie in the back of the SUV. When he saw Cookie driving by an hour later, he wanted to stop the truck to see how Rosie was doing, but he didn't. Time was of the essence and they needed to push the herd as far as they could today.

Dusk was falling, along with the snow, when the first cowboys saw a bright flame.

"Hey, there's camp!" one of them shouted back. Everyone picked up their speed, pushing the herd that much faster. Already four or five inches of snow covered the ground, and a sharp wind blew. They were all looking forward to the heat of the fire.

Jason wanted nothing more than to rush to the campsite to check on Rosie. But he knew a leader didn't put all the work on his men. Instead he asked Nick to ride ahead and bring back news of her condition to everyone. Jason knew he wasn't the only one concerned with her health.

Watching Nick ride ahead when he wanted to be the one was tough on Jason. He kept his gaze fixed on the distant campsite, hoping to see Nick riding back. Finally he saw a rider coming back toward them. He held his position on the herd, until Nick had passed on news to the early riders and got back to him.

"Rosie is keeping soup down now. Tonight she may eat a little bit. She was sitting by the fire. Can you believe it? She was feeling guilty because she rode in the SUV."

"That figures. But she seemed okay?"

"Yeah, I guess. She was helping Cookie cut up some potatoes."

Relief assailed him. "Okay, go with the guys leading the horses. Help them set up the rope corral. By then maybe Cookie will have supper ready. Have them go ahead and eat. You, too. You've done extra duty today. Send the other two back out to the herd. We'll start settling them down. By then maybe the two guys can handle them for a little while."

"Sounds like a plan, boss. After I eat I'll be ready to come back out if I need to. Some of these guys are a little older and may be stiff with the cold and all."

"I appreciate it, Nick, but hopefully we can do without you on the herd until later tonight, at least."

The young cowboy tipped his hat. "I'll go

take care of the horses and get those two guys fed first."

"Thanks." Jason started circling the herd, telling his men to settle the cows down for the night. With six of them, the task went fairly quickly. Then Jason released everyone except Ken. "We'll go into eat when the guys who led the horses come out to relieve us. Is that okay, Ken?"

"Sure, boss. This was easier than riding the hills looking for more cows."

"Yeah, Ken, thanks. We won't be out here too long."

"That's all right. That means we'll appreciate the food more since we have to wait longer."

"Okay. I'll go this way and you go the other."

They had circled the herd almost five times before the other riders came out to relieve them.

Together they rode into camp. They first tended to their horses. Then Ken headed for the fire while Jason looked for Rosie. He found Cookie and asked about her.

"She's lying down in the SUV. She did eat some supper. Just not much."

When Jason turned around to head for the SUV, Cookie asked, "Aren't you going to eat first?"

"No, I want to see Rosie. If you need to clean up, just make me a plate and I'll wash last."

He hurried over to the SUV and opened the front door. Rosie was lying in the back with her eyes closed. He called her softly.

Her eyes fluttered several times before she looked up. "Hi, Jason."

"How are you doing?"

"Fine. I'm sorry I couldn't ride out today."

He couldn't help but smile at her. "Sweetheart, you deserve as much time as you need to recover. I think you had a worse case than the rest of us."

"No. I'm sure I didn't."

How like Rosie to downplay her condition and her earlier contributions. Didn't the woman know she was a born leader?
After all she'd done, she'd deserved a rest, though he was sure she'd balk when he said, "Tomorrow you'll ride to the ranch with Cookie and then Sara Beth will take care of you."

She held true to form and raised her voice

in protest. "I'm not riding in the SUV tomorrow. I'm helping drive the herd to the ranch."

"No, you won't be well enough, Rosie," Jason hurriedly said.

"You are not the boss of me, Jason. It's my herd of cattle and I'll be driving it in. If you want to ride in the SUV, feel free. But I won't!"

He could already see how much the argument was taking out of her. He figured she'd sleep too late and have to ride in the SUV tomorrow. Especially if the horses were taken ahead of the herd.

He reached an arm over the seat and patted her shoulder. "Okay, Rosie, don't get upset. I was just trying to protect you. After all, I promised Wes."

"Good. Then you'll forget about me riding in the SUV."

He smiled at her persistence. "Whatever you say, honey. Just lie down and get some more rest."

That was one suggestion she readily took.

"Did you talk to Rosie?" Cookie asked him as he exited the truck.

"Yeah. And talking to me exhausted her."

"Just talking?" Cookie asked in surprise.

"Well, we had an argument, I guess."

"You shouldn't 'a done that," Cookie said. "She don't have a lot of energy just yet."

"I know that!" Jason was practically yelling. "But the damned woman tried to tell me she would be on horseback in the morning!"

"No wonder you had an argument," Cookie said. "She won't be up to that. She should ride with me. I'll have her back at the house shortly after noon."

Jason frowned. "She's so hardheaded, I won't be surprised if she pulls some stunt and manages to get on horseback."

"But what can we do?"

"I'll try to think of something." He walked with Cookie back to the center of camp, where the older man gave him a heaping plate of meat loaf and vegetables. Jason ate too fast, he knew, but he was starving and cold. As he got hot food inside him and warmed up by the big campfire Cookie had built, he relaxed and ate the rest of his meal more slowly.

"What are you gonna do to keep Rosie from riding tomorrow?" Nick asked.

"I'm hoping she'll sleep late in the morning and we can take the extra horses ahead of the cattle."

"Uh, Jason, I don't want to be assigned the horses in the morning," Nick hurriedly said.

Not making the connection, Jason gave him a puzzled look. "Why not, Nick?"

"Um, I don't want Rosie mad at me."

"Oh. Okay, I'll find someone else to do the dirty deed."

They all ate silently. When Jason, the last to finish, washed his plate, Nick said, "I didn't really mean that, Jason. But you know she will be mad if she intends to ride out in the morning."

"She really does, but even arguing about it exhausted her." Jason sighed. "I don't know what I'll do if she wakes up early."

"We'll help you, boss, won't we, guys?"

There was a general consensus that the men could talk Rosie out of mounting her horse in the morning, but Jason had a feeling they were wrong.

Jason was up at first light, as was Cookie. He helped get the fire ready and did Rosie's job of cracking and beating the eggs for breakfast. When he brought the bowl to Cookie, he whispered, "Did Rosie wake up when you got out of the SUV?"

"I don't think so."

"Good. I'm not going to go check and see. I'm hoping she'll sleep until after we get the herd started."

"Yeah. Uh, you want to wake up the others so they can eat their breakfasts?" Cookie asked.

Jason moved around the campfire, shaking shoulders to awaken the cowboys. He'd just finished making the circle when the SUV door opened and Rosemary got out, with her coat and hat on.

"Rosie! I thought you'd sleep a little later," Jason said.

"Why? We always start early." She moved to the campfire, holding out her hands to its warmth. "It's still snowing."

"Yeah, we picked up another three or four inches overnight. That's why you should ride with Cookie. He might need help if he gets stuck." That idea had just occurred to him. He hoped it worked.

"I assumed the two men who rode the herd all night would ride with Cookie."

"How did you know—" But there was no fooling Rosie. No use even trying. He admitted, "Yeah, they are."

"Then there's no need for me to ride with him."

"No, but—" Jason broke off, unable to think of anything else spur of the moment.

"Hey, Rosie, I figured you'd be riding with Cookie. That's why I didn't tell you Maggie came up limping yesterday," Nick offered.

Jason sent him a grateful look.

"Then I'll ride Sandy."

The two men stared at each other.

"Are you sure you feel strong enough to stay upright in the saddle all day?" Cookie asked.

"I will after I have a good breakfast," she answered him.

"Okay, we'll see. But there's no shame riding in the SUV with me."

"With the night guys riding with you, Cookie, and two guys leading the spare horses, that will only leave six of us to bring the herd in. I think I'll be needed."

"But we could manage if you don't feel up to it," Jason hurriedly said.

"I can manage."

"First you got to keep down a good breakfast, Rosie," Cookie reminded her.

All the men looked at each other, guiltily hoping she couldn't do that.

CHAPTER NINE

ROSEMARY couldn't imagine a stranger breakfast. As she struggled to eat, every cowboy was staring at her, waiting for her to be sick. She took small bites and swallowed slowly. If a person could control their stomach, Rosemary intended to be the one who did it.

When she'd eaten about half of what Cookie had given her, she dumped the rest in the slop bucket and excused herself. She knew all of them would give her some privacy. When she reached the trees that would hide her activity, she gave up the rigid control of her stomach and shakily lost some of her breakfast. But no one would know. She was determined about that.

When she reached camp again, Jason met her. "Are you all right?"

"Yes, of course."

"It really would be best if you stayed with Cookie in the SUV."

"No, Jason. I told you last night I was riding with the herd today. And I'm not going to argue with you." She moved around him and headed for the horses. Nick surprised her by leading Maggie to her.

"I thought you said she was limping?"

"Uh, I think she recovered overnight."

Rosemary gave him a derisive look before she thanked him for saddling her horse. She looked around camp, wondering if she could get in the saddle as gracefully as she usually did. She knew everyone would be watching her. If she asked Nick for help, Jason would insist she ride in the SUV.

Suddenly she felt hands around her waist. She looked up to find Jason standing beside her.

"Need a little help?"

"If I do, will you insist I ride in the truck?"

"No, Rosie, I've accepted your decision."

She sighed softly. "Then yes, please, I could use some help."

"Here we go," he said as he lifted her. All Rosemary had to do was throw her leg over Maggie and settle down in the saddle.

"Thank you," she said, hating the breathlessness in her voice. She didn't want Jason to think his touch mattered to her. "I appreciate the help."

Jason put his hand on her leg, to ensure she didn't ride off. "You'll be riding drag with me."

"You don't have to stay beside me, Jason."

His tone brooked no argument. "We'll ride together, Rosie, or you'll ride in the truck. Your choice."

She stared him down for the final time, then huffed, "Fine!"

"Don't forget to get your sandwich from Cookie."

"I have been on roundups before, Jason."

"Wait!" Jason suddenly said, startling her.

"What?"

"You don't have your slicker on. Where is it?"

She reached behind her to her saddlebags and drew out the yellow plastic cover to keep her dry. "I forgot to put it on. I'll do that now."

He kept Maggie in place as Rosemary shrugged her slicker over her coat. The plastic kept out the cold wind, and Rosemary was grateful to Jason for reminding her. "Thank you again. Now may I go?"

"Get your sandwich," he reminded her.

"Do you think I'm simple-minded, Jason? We've already had this conversation." She pulled Maggie from his hold and headed toward the SUV.

"Cookie, do you have the sandwiches ready?"

"Sure do, Rosie. Are you sure—"

"Don't start, Cookie. I'm fine, thanks to your good care. I'll see you back at the ranch. You certainly did a good job."

"Thanks, Rosie. Be careful."

"Always," Rosie said with a smile, though she was shaking inside. She turned her horse toward the herd and drew a deep breath.

When she reached the herd, she relieved one of the cowboys who would ride to the ranch in the truck. He wanted to pull a double shift, but Rosie assured him he'd done his job. Now she would do hers.

She saw Nick relieve the other man. Immediately following Nick were several other cowboys. It was time to start moving the herd. She hoped they moved them quickly, before she fell out of her saddle.

Jason hurried to saddle his horse. The anxiety he felt at being apart from Rosie was growing. Soon he'd be following her around with his tongue hanging out. He wasn't even sure she'd notice.

He picked up his sandwich from Cookie and said goodbye. He visually checked the camp for any details he might've missed. Then he rode toward the herd. He noted Nick was on point on this side to keep the herd headed in the right direction. Ken was on the other side. They were good riders.

The herd was shaped roughly in a triangle. Rosie was already at the base of the triangle, pushing the herd forward. Jason joined her.

"You could've waited for me," he teased.

"No time. We've got to get moving," she assured him, not even offering him a smile.

He shrugged his shoulders and joined her efforts. He hoped she didn't notice how closely he stuck to her while still trying to do his job. When several steers with a mind of their own broke from the herd, he rode after them in hot pursuit.

As he headed back to the herd, the steers in front of him, he turned his gaze toward the back of the herd to search for Rosie. When he didn't see her, he panicked, spurring on his horse, which forced the steers to run faster. Then he caught sight of her on the far side of the herd. He eased his pace, drawing deep breaths to calm down.

Man, he needed to take things slower.

"You okay?" he called to Rosie as soon as he got close to her.

She just waved at him and turned away. He frowned. Was she too tired to speak? Or too sick? He considered riding closer, but he had a job to do, as did she, and he had no choice but to postpone his concern.

About three o'clock, one of the cowboys on point yelled that they'd reached the pasture where they were to leave the herd. Two riders came out to meet them. They turned out to be Rafe and Jesse. Everyone greeted them joyfully, both in relief for the roundup to be over and to let them know they were glad to see them.

Nick and Ken remained at the gate that led into the pasture to keep any cows from trying to resist their entry, but as the herd entered the pasture and found hay waiting for them, they moved quickly. As they did, Rafe and Jesse came to Jason.

"Boss, Nick said to relieve you and Rosie. You can take her to the house. Sara Beth is worrying herself to a frazzle. Rosie is her only chick, you know."

"Okay, thanks, guys," Jason agreed. He turned and rode toward Rosie.

"I'm fine!" she called out.

Did she think that would stop him? Jason shook his head, but he didn't turn back. "Come on, Rosie. Rafe and Jesse are relieving us. Sara Beth wants to see you at once."

"But we need to put out hay and—"

"Jesse and Rafe have already done that. That's why the herd is moving so quickly. Let's go." He reached down to take her bridle to lead her horse.

"Stop that! I can guide my horse!"

He saw the stubbornness on her face, but he also saw the exhaustion. "Come on, Rosie. I was just trying to help."

"I know, but I can make it."

He removed his hand and sat back in his saddle. "Sorry. I'm as anxious as Sara Beth about your health."

She drew a deep breath. "That's not your job."

He wanted to tell her it was his job for life, if she'd only agree. But now was not the time. He needed to take time to be sure about what he wanted. After all, he'd already messed up once.

When they reached the barn, he convinced her to ride right up to the back door of the ranch house. As they came to a halt, Sara Beth bolted through the door before they'd even dismounted. Jason swung from the saddle and went to help Rosie from the saddle.

"I can make it," she said.

"No need. I'm here. You've proven yourself over and over again, Rosie. It's time to let Sara Beth take care of you." As he spoke, he pulled Rosie from the saddle and into his arms.

"Oh my, thank you, Jason," Sara Beth said. "Bring her right this way."

He wasn't sure where Sara Beth would lead him, but he followed her without question, carrying Rosie in his arms. She'd given up protesting, he noticed. The warmth of the kitchen hit him as he entered. It was a good feeling.

"Put her down here. I'll give her some coffee and juice first," Sara Beth said.

Jason found Wes sitting by the table, his casted leg propped up in the chair next to him.

"How are you doing?" Jason asked him as he eased Rosie into a chair across from Wes.

"I'm good. Have a seat, Jason."

"Thanks, I'll take you up on that in a few minutes. I need to take our horses to the corral and make sure they get some hay."

"One of the boys can't do that?" Wes asked.

"They're busy. I won't be long."

"Okay. We'll have the coffee hot and waiting for you."

"Thanks."

When he got back to the house half an hour later, he stood outside and knocked on the door. Sara Beth finally opened it. "My goodness, Jason. No need to knock. Just come on in."

"Thanks, Sara Beth. I didn't want to startle you."

"I'll pour you a cup of coffee. I bet you're half frozen."

"Pretty much," he agreed with a smile. "How's Rosie?"

"She's upstairs taking a hot shower. That's what she asked to do first. Then I'll put her to bed with some medicine."

"She probably needs to eat something. She hasn't eaten much in the last couple of days."

"I know. I found her sandwich uneaten in her coat pocket. She said she forgot to eat it. I made her try to eat some of it with her coffee. She managed a little bit."

"We tried to keep her from riding today," Jason said as he sat down at the table across from Wes.

"Not an easy task," Wes drawled with a smile. "She's got her daddy's strong will. Makes up her own mind."

"Yeah, I discovered that. The cowboys are all in the bunkhouse now, Wes. We didn't have any more accidents once we got rid of Ted. Have you talked to the sheriff about him?"

"Sure. Ted's long gone, after explaining he was trying to help you disrupt the roundup so you'd get the ranch."

Jason froze. Then he looked at Wes. "I swear he's lying, Wes. I would never do something so low-down!"

"I figured it wasn't your idea. But I can believe it was Ted's way of insuring he had a job."

Jason sank back in his chair in relief. "Yeah, I can see that, too. But why did the sheriff release him?"

"He said I didn't have any proof, so he couldn't hold him."

"And he couldn't wait until we got back?"

"Sheriff said when we had proof to bring it in and he'd put a warrant out on Ted. But we'd have to have hard proof."

"What did you tell him?"

"I said I'd wait until you got back and discuss it with you."

Jason rubbed the back of his neck as he thought about what Wes had said. With a sigh, he said, "I don't think we have enough proof. But when I get back to Denver, I'm going to call the man who gave him such a glowing recommendation and let him know what it was worth."

Wes nodded.

"But other than that," Jason added, "I don't know what we can do."

"Don't worry about it. I talked it over with Jesse and Rafe. They feel the same way I do. The man was scum and you made a mistake. But you corrected it as soon as you realized what was happening."

"Sounds to me you're letting me off easy."

Wes smiled at him. "Well, we won't fight you if you want to pay our medical bills—the part that our insurance doesn't cover."

"Done. But what else can I do?"

"Keep all of us on when you take over the ranch."

Jason stared at Wes and then leaned forward. "I'm not getting the ranch. We brought in more than two hundred head of cows, just like Rosie said."

"You did? But Rosie told us you were taking over. She said that just before she went upstairs."

"Why did she say that?" Jason asked, confused.

"I'm not sure," Wes said slowly. He turned to stare at his wife, working across the room. "Sara Beth? Why do you think Rosie said she was losing the ranch?"

"I don't know. And you're not going to ask her right now. She's weak and needs to rest."

Wes shrugged his shoulders. "Okay. You got something Jason and I can snack on? Like some cake or something?"

Though she made a tsking sound, Sara Beth immediately cut them each a big piece of chocolate cake. "Maybe this will hold you until supper," she said with a smile. "I'm taking a piece up to Rosie now."

Jason wanted to offer to do that task, but he had to settle for his piece of chocolate cake.

When he finished, he stood. "Wes, thanks for believing me."

"Sure, Jason. Now, where do you think you're going?"

"I figured I'd load up my horses and head for Denver."

"I think it would be better for you to spend the night tonight and head back to Denver in the morning, when you're a little fresher."

With a sigh, Jason said, "You're probably right. Where's the closest motel?"

"Right here. We've got plenty of bedrooms upstairs. Sara Beth assumed you'd want to spend the night. She's already got one prepared for you."

"I don't think I should cause her so much work. She's already got Rosie to take care of."

About that time, Sara Beth entered the kitchen, an empty saucer in her hand. "Look, I got Rosie to eat her cake. Now she's gone to sleep." She beamed at them before she noticed Jason standing. "Is something wrong?"

"Jason thinks he should go to a motel tonight," Wes explained.

Sara Beth looked at him in surprise. "But I've already prepared a room for you, Jason. Surely you'd prefer to stay here instead of some motel," she said, making the word motel sound like a rattrap.

"It's not that I wouldn't like to stay, but I figure you've got your hands full with Rosie."

"Nonsense! I could take care of her with one hand behind my back. Besides, I had a vacation while you all were on the roundup. Please stay with us."

"Thank you, Sara Beth. I'd be pleased to stay," Jason said.

"You take your bag up to the first room on the right. It's across the hall from Rosie's room. It has a connecting bath, too, like hers."

"Thanks. I'll go get my bag from the bunkhouse and be right back."

A few minutes later, he passed through the kitchen and headed upstairs. When he reached the top, he stood there, staring at the door across the hall from his. Rosie's room. He put down his bag and softly rapped on her door.

There was no answer.

He slowly turned the knob and saw Rosie curled up under the cover, peacefully sleeping. He wondered if she'd get up for supper and come to the table. He hoped so. Or at least breakfast in the morning.

When he heard footsteps at the bottom of the stairs, he hurriedly closed Rosie's door and opened his own across the hall.

Sara Beth appeared on the landing. "Oh, Jason, I just wanted to be sure you didn't need anything."

"I'm sure I don't, Sara Beth. The room looks wonderful," he said, smiling.

"I hope that's true. Supper will be ready in about half an hour."

"Okay. Will Rosie come down to supper?"

"I'm going to wake her up and encourage her to come down, but it depends on how she feels. Hopefully she will."

"I hope so, too. I'd like to see her again before I leave."

She smiled at him. "We'll see."

He had nothing left to do but to enter his room and close the door. The draw of a hot shower had him undressing at once. He felt like it had been months since he'd enjoyed a good hot shower. Nothing like a roundup to make you appreciate the conveniences, he thought.

Half an hour later, he was back downstairs in the kitchen, smelling a lot better than he had before. Wes and Sara Beth were there, too, but no Rosie.

Just as he was about to ask, the door opened again and Rosie came into the kitchen. She hugged Sara Beth, and then Wes. After that, she took her place at the table across from the ranch manager.

"Evening," Jason said, watching Rosie closely to see her reaction. Hadn't she noticed his presence?

She finally looked at him, though only briefly enough to reply, "Evening, Jason." Then she turned to Wes. "How's your foot? I forgot to ask earlier."

"My foot's fine, Rosie. How are you feeling? You looked kind of pale when you first got here."

"I'm fine. I was just tired."

"And still a little sick, I think," Jason added.

"No, I'm well," she said stiffly, avoiding his gaze.

"Well, now, Rosie," Wes began, "I think you have to appreciate Jason's concern, even if you don't think you deserve it."

Rosemary's gaze jerked up to Wes's face. Then, with reluctance, it seemed to Jason, she faced him. "Wes is right. I should appreciate the care you gave me after Wes left."

"Should?" Sara Beth asked. "The man was following my orders, and I think he did a good job."

"Yes, fine. He did a good job. Thank you, Jason."

"That's my girl," Sara Beth crooned, a smile on her face.

Wes raised his eyebrows, but he didn't say anything.

Sara Beth began bringing dishes to the table. Jason hadn't exactly suffered bad food on the roundup, thanks to Cookie, who had done a good job of feeding them in difficult circumstances, but Sara Beth's dinner smelled and looked like heaven.

Jason accepted a portion of almost everything, especially the hot biscuits. He tried to eat slowly, but the feast overpowered him. Finally he wiped his face with his napkin and looked at Sara Beth.

"That was the best dinner I've ever eaten, Sara Beth. Thank you."

"Now, Jason, I know you've dined in really nice restaurants in Denver. I'm sure—"

"Never one as good as this, I promise."

She smiled broadly. "Well, I thank you. It's good someone appreciated all my cooking," she said, staring at Rosemary.

"I tried, Sara Beth. It all tasted really good, but my stomach is still a little queasy." Rosemary tried her best smile on Sara Beth.

Jason thought if she gave him that kind of smile, he'd snatch her out of her chair and charge up the stairs to the nearest bedroom. But she'd avoided his eyes all evening, so it wasn't likely to happen.

He decided it was time to take the bit in his teeth and ask Rosie why she'd said the ranch would be his. After all, he'd busted his butt to be sure she got to keep her home. It was time to straighten out the mystery. He opened his mouth, but Wes must've been watching him. He cut him off.

"Rosie, I think it's time you went to bed. You need a full night's sleep. Sara Beth, you want to take her to bed?"

It was more a command than a request, and neither woman resisted.

Jason stared after Rosie with intense longing in his gaze.

Wes shook him from his thoughts. "Jason, you can't ask Rosie the question about the ranch until in the morning. She's not strong enough now. Besides, I want to see the herd before you ask her."

"Why?"

"Just to satisfy my own mind. It's hard to believe you have two hundred head of cattle until I see them."

"Well, Wes, it's going to be kind of difficult since you can't ride a horse yet."

"Don't worry, boy. I've got it all planned."

CHAPTER TEN

AFTER a good night's sleep, Jason was up by six-thirty. He dressed and crept to the door, trying to figure out if anyone in the house was up.

He could hear nothing, so he opened his door and stepped out into the hall. He heard movement downstairs. Stepping closer to Rosie's door, he listened for sounds of life in her room. Either she was already down, or she was sleeping in.

With a shrug of his shoulders, he went down the stairs. In the kitchen, he discovered Wes and Sara Beth, talking quietly at the kitchen table.

The minute she noticed Jason, Sara Beth welcomed him into the kitchen and got up to fix his breakfast.

"You can wait until Rosie gets up, Sara Beth," Jason said. "No need to cook twice more this morning."

"It's not a problem, Jason. And Rosie is sleeping in this morning. You know, it takes a while to let go after a stressful situation."

"Of course. I appreciate the breakfast. Cookie was good, but you're even better, Sara Beth."

"Oh, Jason, I love your flattery," Sara Beth said with a big grin.

"Watch it, Jason," Wes protested. "I won't have you sweet-talking my woman."

Jason wondered how he'd feel about Jason trying to sweet-talk Rosie. He suspected Wes considered himself her father figure. Would he have to ask Wes for permission to marry Rosie?

"Do you want to go see the herd as soon as I finish breakfast, Wes?" He figured a change of subject would be good.

"Yeah, as soon as you're finished."

"How are you going to get there?"

"We've got a truck that can go there, if you'll get out and open the gates."

"No problem," Jason assured him. Sara Beth set a plate full of eggs, bacon and fried potatoes in front of him. She added a pan full of biscuits.

"That's a lot of food, Sara Beth. Especially the biscuits."

"I could help you with the biscuits," Wes

said softly. "Sara Beth made some apple jelly that tastes real good on a biscuit."

Jason smiled. "I'll share the biscuits if you'll share the jelly," he said to Wes.

"You've got a deal," Wes agreed. He said it softly as if he didn't want Sara Beth to know.

Jason looked over his shoulder. Sara Beth was staring at the pair of them. He smiled at her and then turned back to his breakfast. When he took a biscuit, he nudged the plate closer to Wes.

After a filling breakfast and no sign of Rosie, Jason was ready to go look at the cows. Jason grabbed his coat and bundled up again. Less than twenty-four hours of warmth and he didn't want to get out in the cold again.

Wes pointed out a truck parked next to the house. "This is the truck Sara Beth drove to pick me up. Boy, was I glad to see her that day! I was aching all over!"

"Yeah. It was good that Rosie thought of that."

"She's a smart little girl," Wes agreed with a grin.

"I don't think of her as a little girl," Jason said, looking at Wes out of the corner of his eye after they got into the truck.

Wes pointed south. "Drive over there."

Jason did as he said, wondering if Wes would say anything about his remark.

"I never thought you did," Wes said softly.

"No, I guess I was pretty obvious, but Rosie doesn't seem to have noticed."

"That's probably why she said you'd get the ranch."

"I don't follow you, Wes. Why would my getting the ranch make such a difference?"

"I don't know. Who can figure out a woman's mind?"

"Do I need to tell you I'm serious? I'm offering marriage, not an affair or anything like that." He'd made that decision overnight.

Wes grinned. "Good. I'd hate to have to knock your block off," he said. "I promised her daddy I'd take care of her."

"I figured. What do I do now?"

"About what?"

Jason frowned. This conversation wasn't going well. "Will you talk to her...or should I?"

"Lord'a mercy, boy! You don't know?"

"Last night you didn't want me to talk to her about saying the ranch was mine. I didn't want to do anything you were against."

"I just felt she was too tired to know what she was saying. You go on back to Denver and I'll figure it all out. Then I'll call you and let you know."

"You want me to go back without seeing her?" Jason asked, his voice rising.

"I think that's best. You did behave yourself on the roundup, didn't you?"

"I may have kissed her once or twice, but—but it wasn't anything important." Jason could feel his cheeks flushing.

"Kissed her? What did she say?"

"Nothing. It was usually when she was upset about something and—and she didn't say anything about it."

Wes gave him a sharp look. Then he looked toward the herd. "Okay, I guess you're not in my black book."

"I'm glad."

"You're right," Wes said.

Jason's heart raced. What did Wes mean? Did he think Rosie cared about him?

"I do believe you've brought back about two hundred and thirty head of cows."

"Oh, uh, yeah, I think that's about right."

"So Rosie should be able to keep the ranch."

"Right." That hadn't been the most important thought in Jason's mind, but he could accept that.

"Okay, we'll get them to market and Rosie will repay your down payment. You're okay with that?"

"Yes, of course. That was our agreement."

"Well, then, you'd best go pack and be on your way."

"I don't get to see Rosie before I go? I could ask her—"

"No. If you're still serious, you can talk to her after the question about the ranch is answered. Better not to mix romance with business. I did that once and lost a mighty fine girl. 'Course, it worked out well because I got Sara Beth. But I don't want Rosie hurt."

Jason guessed he was right, but it didn't feel right, leaving without at least telling Rosie goodbye. All the way back to the house, he hoped and prayed he'd see Rosie…just for a few minutes. Just to say goodbye.

No such luck.

Jason thanked Sara Beth for her hospitality and asked her to tell Rosie goodbye. Though there was so much he wanted to say to Rosie, none of it could go through an intermediary, even one as nice as Sara Beth. After all, what woman wanted to hear a man say "I love you" from someone else?

And he did love Rosie.

With a longing glance up the stairs, he left the ranch house. Losing the Bar G didn't bother him anymore. The prospect of losing Rosie did.

Pulling down on his hat, he rode away, towing his horse trailer. His fate rested in Wes's hands.

* * *

Rosemary slowly came down the stairs. It was almost nine o'clock. She couldn't believe she'd slept so late. Was Jason still here? Would he be sitting at the kitchen table with Wes and Sara Beth? She couldn't decide what she wished for.

The choice was taken out of her hands when she opened the kitchen door and Sara Beth was the only person in sight. She swallowed the disappointment and cheerfully said, "Good morning."

Sara Beth spun around. "Rosie, are you feeling all right?"

"Yes. I'm sorry I slept so late. Where's …Wes?"

"Oh, he's down visiting with the cowboys,

of course. He wanted to hear all about the roundup after he left. He said it looks like you brought back about two hundred and thirty head. That was a good job."

As she talked, Sara Beth had filled a mug of hot coffee for Rosemary and set it in front of her.

"Oh. Didn't Jason fill him in?" Since Sara Beth hadn't mentioned Jason, she would. Maybe she'd get more information. After Jason's care of her, and his reckless promise, she'd hoped—

"Of course, but he wanted to hear from the men, too. Besides, I think he wanted to sneak some more breakfast from Cookie!" Sara Beth said, her hands on her hips.

"Didn't he have breakfast here?"

"Of course. And then he shared some of Jason's before they went to look at the cows. But his appetite has increased instead of decreased since he broke his ankle."

"Oh, is Jason with Wes?" She worked hard to keep her voice even, as if it didn't matter either way.

"No, after they checked out the cattle, Jason loaded up his horses and headed for Denver." Sara Beth broke some eggs to scramble. "He said to tell you goodbye."

Rosemary felt as if she'd been hit broadside by a two-ton steer. All the breath whooshed out of her. She put her head down, staring into her coffee as if it was worthy of intense interest. She said nothing. What could she say? That Jason had kissed her, promised her more when they returned? But he'd also told her they'd had to present a united front out on the roundup....

It all came clear to her now. Jason was pretending. The kisses she'd taken as real were nothing but a pretense, a ruse to make her go along with his plan to dupe the cowboys.

She should have known. For a man like Jason Barton, who had women dropping at his feet—women like the one she'd met back in Denver—a few kisses and a promise meant nothing. He could get whatever he wanted from any of a hundred gorgeous, leggy, busty women back home.

Well, she scoffed, they were welcome to him!

Sara Beth sounded concerned when she said, "Anything wrong, Rosie?"

She looked up, a fake smile pasted on her face.

"No, of course not." What could be wrong? She'd fallen for a millionaire who had left her as soon as his responsibility had ended. Just what she should've expected.

After a moment of silence, Sara Beth said, "That Jason is one handsome guy, isn't he? You did notice, didn't you?"

"Yes, I noticed." She pretended disinterest. "But he's a millionaire and I suspect he's not hurting for company in Denver."

Sara Beth brought over Rosie's breakfast. Then she poured herself another mug of coffee and sat down at the table with Rosie.

"You fell for him, didn't you?" Sara Beth asked softly.

There was no use denying it. Sara Beth had always had the ability to see right through Rosie, ever since she was a little girl with a big problem on her mind.

Rosemary nodded but said nothing. She was afraid she'd start crying if she spoke.

"He seemed concerned about you," Sara Beth said.

After swallowing hard, she finally said, "Yes, he was very intent on the roundup, once Wes left. He mostly took over and tried to order me around!" That wasn't exactly accurate, but she had to work up some anger to keep her composure.

Sara Beth patted her hand. "Eat your breakfast, honey."

Rosie took a bite of scrambled egg, but she wasn't enthusiastic.

"Was that why you said he had earned the ranch?"

Rosemary kept her head down, stirring the scrambled eggs, as if she were cooking them. "I realized...I'm not cut out to be a ranch owner. Even if I made enough to pay him back his down payment, I'm not sure I can come up with the money for the payroll for the winter." She sniffed several times, still not raising her head.

"Oh, honey, we don't want you to lose the ranch."

"I can't make it work," Rosie said, her voice rising with emotion. Then she broke into tears and lay her head on her folded arms, shoving her breakfast aside.

Sara Beth jumped up and circled the table to take Rosemary in her arms. "Shh, honey, don't cry. We'll work something out."

Rosemary sobbed even more, knowing the dream she'd had of keeping her home had ended. She couldn't put everyone connected with the ranch in danger of not receiving their wages. In the beginning, she'd thought they could pay back Jason's down payment and maybe make it until spring. But with snow already on the ground, she wouldn't be able to even buy the hay to make it through the winter, let alone make payroll. She might not even be able to buy the groceries to make it until spring.

And she was tired.

Out on the roundup, she'd realized she didn't have the strength to lead her men. They were great, and Wes was strong, as he should be, but she had failed the test of strength.

When Wes had gone down, Jason had stepped in. She'd only been a figurehead.

Rosemary had tried to equal the men in her determination and strength, but she hadn't succeeded.

When Wes came in fifteen minutes later, Sara Beth had mopped up the tears and encouraged Rosie to eat more of her breakfast.

"Well, there's our Sleeping Beauty," Wes said jovially, smiling at Rosie.

"Good morning, Wes," she replied quietly. "How are the men?"

"They're all fine and singing your praises to the sky."

Rosemary stared at him. "Me?"

"A 'course, you. They said you made them all feel weak and lazy. You rode herd all night even though you were throwing up.

They'd all gone down at the first hint of a sick stomach."

"That's because men don't have to experience childbearing!" Sara Beth said with a sniff.

"I guess you're right, sweetheart. But Rosie did us proud!"

"No, I didn't. I wasn't nearly as strong as anyone. And it was Jason who brought the herd home and kept an eye on me, too. I don't deserve anyone's praise!" And she jumped up and ran from the room.

Wes stared at the door as it swung to. "Did I say something wrong?"

"Obviously," his wife responded. "Rosie is feeling she let everyone down and that she's not strong enough to handle running the ranch."

"But I'm here to help her! I never thought she should run the ranch all by herself."

"I think she needs more rest. I'll go see if she's gone back to bed." Sara Beth slipped up the stairs and rapped softly on Rosie's door.

When there was no answer, she quietly opened the door and saw Rosie sleeping on her bed. Sara Beth pulled the cover over Rosie and tiptoed out of the room.

"Wes? It's Jason. How's Rosie?"

"Well, hi there, Jason. You get to Denver all right?"

"Yeah, Wes, but I need to know how Rosie is doing."

"She's doing better. Sara Beth is taking care of her. I got the herd sent off to market. She should get a check soon. Then you can clear up the question of the ranch."

"I'm not worried about that, Wes."

"I know, boy, but it's better to keep business and emotion separate."

"May I speak to Rosie?"

"She's taking a nap, Jason. She still hasn't recovered from the roundup yet."

"Wes, it's been over a week. Maybe she should see a doctor."

"I'll talk to Sara Beth about it. She seems to think that Rosie was making it on nerves before the roundup even started, what with her dad dying and all, and she really overextended herself. But we'll talk about it."

"Will you tell Rosie I called to see how she's doing?"

"Sure thing. I'll do that."

"All right. Thanks, Wes."

"No problem. Thanks for calling."

"Hey, Rosie, the check came for the sale of the herd you brought back," Wes said as Rosemary entered the kitchen a few days later.

He handed the envelope to her and she slowly opened it. Rosemary stared at the check. The amount was a few thousand over the required fifty thousand dollars to Jason back. She slid it across the table so Wes could see it.

"So you're going to return the down payment?"

She slowly shook her head. "It wouldn't leave enough to make it through the winter, Wes. You know that. I'm going to let the sale go through. You and Sara Beth will be okay, and the rest of the staff. They're all good."

"Yes, they are, but they want you back. As much as they enjoyed working with Jason, they're loyal to you."

Rosemary let her head hang down. "I don't deserve their loyalty."

"That's not true, Rosie," Wes said. "You got sick, like everyone else, but you kept going. I think they feel guilty that they left it all up to you."

Rosemary stood and began pacing the kitchen. "I can't keep the ranch, Wes. Jason will have the money to keep it going even if he has a bad year. I would be on such a tight budget that even if I worked nonstop, it would only take one crisis to send me under. You know that."

"So you're just going to walk away?" Wes asked.

She nodded her head.

"You going to call Jason and tell him?"

"No. I'll send him a letter. He can reinstate the closing and let me know."

Wes exchanged a worried frown with his wife, but he said nothing else.

That night, after Rosemary and Sara Beth had retired for the night, Wes called Jason at home. "Jason, it's Wes."

"Is everything all right?" Jason asked urgently.

"Yeah, but Rosie got the check today."

"Was it enough to pay me back?"

"Yeah, but she said she's going to write you

a letter that she can't make the payment and that the sale can go through."

"Why?"

"She says she wouldn't have enough funds to make it through the winter. She knows you can keep the ranch going. She thinks she's doing us all a favor by giving up the ranch."

"I'll be there tomorrow," Jason said. "Ask Sara Beth if I can stay for a day or two, until we get this straightened out."

"I'll ask her, but I know she'll say it's okay. Come on ahead."

"Thanks, Wes. I'll see you tomorrow for lunch."

Because Rosie still wasn't making it down to breakfast early in the morning, Wes could inform his wife about his phone call to Jason after she'd gone to bed last night.

"Of course he can stay as long as he wants," Sara Beth said. "What did Rosie say about it?"

Wes concentrated on his breakfast, but his wife prodded him. "Well?"

"Uh, I haven't told Rosie yet."

"Wes! What do you mean? You're going to tell her, aren't you?"

"Well, now, Sara Beth, I think it might be good to take Rosie by surprise. You know, not give her time to prepare a speech."

"Shame on you, Wes. Rosie doesn't make up things. She always faces what comes and gives her best."

"Yeah, but I think Jason wants to talk to her about more than the ranch. It's better if we don't tell her."

Sara Beth wagged a finger at him. "You'd better be right. I don't want Rosie upset."

"So, what are we having for lunch?" Wes asked, knowing his best option was to get his wife thinking about what she'd prepare instead of thinking about Rosie.

Just then Rosie came downstairs, carrying a letter in her hand. "Will you mail this for me, Wes?"

"Sure, I'll take care of it. It's addressed to Jason? You're letting him know he can have the ranch?"

"Yes."

"Here's your breakfast, honey," Sara Beth said, setting a full plate in front of Rosemary.

"Oh, Sara Beth, I don't think I can eat all of this."

"Just try, Rosie. You have to start eating more.

You're losing weight, and you're getting too thin."

"In the city, they say you can never be too thin," Rosie said listlessly.

"But you live here, on the ranch, and right now a strong wind would blow you away," Sara Beth pointed out.

Raising sad eyes to look at Sara Beth, Rosemary said, "But I won't be living here much longer, you know."

"Oh, honey," Sara Beth crooned and reached out to hug the only child she'd ever had to worry over.

"I'm okay, Sara Beth, I promise. It will just take a little adjustment."

"But surely it will take some time, won't it?"

"Yes, a few weeks, but I need to find a job."

"You'll go back to Cheyenne?"

"That's the closest place for me to work and…and maybe be able to visit you occasionally."

"Wes said he mentioned it to Jason and he said you could visit whenever you wanted. That was generous of him."

"Yes," Rosemary agreed, wondering if she'd be capable of visiting without breaking her heart every time. She felt so silly, mooning around about a man who had had no difficulty leaving her. He hadn't even bothered to write her a note.

Rosemary had held out hope that Jason had come to feel something other than responsibility for her. But as the days passed, she knew that wasn't true. She'd come to realize even hoping to impress Jason had been a ridiculous thought.

She'd lost her family ranch…and she'd lost her heart.

And now she needed to get on with her life.

"I've been sorting through my wardrobe, Sara Beth. I have a lot of clothes to give to charity. Do you know anyone in the area in need of clothes?"

"Yes, the church tries to keep donated clothes on hand, but they have used most of what they had. But are you sure—"

"Yes, I'm sure. Can you look at my pile of clothes to see what you think they can use?"

"Yes, I can do that after lunch. But I'm sure you can leave what you don't need in the city here for when you come back."

"No. Jason will probably bring friends here to visit frequently. After all, I'm sure he'll have a lot of people wanting to spend time with him." She managed a smile. "And it won't be my home any longer."

After Rosemary left the kitchen, Sara Beth returned to her cooking. She wanted to please Jason, but she felt loyal to Rosie. If only Jason could come to care about Rosie. Then she could have her love and her ranch.

Sara Beth had thought about talking to her husband about Rosie's love for Jason, but her husband didn't put much emphasis on a woman's emotions. So she'd been keeping Rosie's secret ever since her return.

Wes and Sara Beth were in the kitchen when they heard a vehicle pull into the driveway. They exchanged a glance and Sara Beth hurried to the window.

"It's him. Oh, no!" Sara Beth exclaimed.

"What's wrong?" Wes demanded, reaching for his crutches.

"He—he's brought a woman with him!"

CHAPTER ELEVEN

SARA BETH spun around and clapped a hand over her mouth.

Wes coughed. "Uh, I think we've got visitors."

Rosemary asked, "Who is it?"

But neither replied by the time Rosie heard a knock on the back door.

"I guess I'll find out," she said as she moved to the door.

She'd expected someone from Blue Ridge, the small town near them. Maybe one of Sara Beth's church friends. She never expected Jason.

And he was with a woman. A beautiful young woman. And another man. She felt like running to her room and slamming the door, but instead, she pasted a smile on her face.

"Come in. Jason, I didn't know you were coming."

He shot a tenuous look at Wes. "Uh, yeah, I talked to Wes yesterday and he invited me to drop in for lunch whenever."

"I see," Rosemary said when she really didn't. One didn't just pop in from Denver, about six hours away. Why was he here? "And you brought friends?"

"Yes, this is Marion and Doug Lock. They're friends of mine from Denver."

"How do you do? Won't you come in? I think Sara Beth has lunch ready." Amazing timing, was all Rosemary could think. It certainly didn't improve her appetite.

"Thank you," Marion replied. "We appreciate your hospitality."

Rosemary led them in and made the introductions, trying hard not to let her emotions get the best of her. When she went to add three places at the table, she noticed that the table was already set for four. She frowned, realizing Sara Beth had already planned for Jason for lunch.

Obviously he hadn't gotten her letter already. And why would he come even if he had? Did he want to move in early? She turned to look at Sara Beth, but the woman kept her gaze on the platters she was setting on the tables.

"May I help?" Marion asked, appearing at Sara Beth's side.

She turned to the woman. Tall, rail thin and blond, Marion flashed a white-toothed smile that had no doubt been chemically enhanced. Despite the long drive, her wool suit looked fresh and new. Rosie wanted to hate her on sight, but she had to admit the woman seemed friendly enough.

"Why, thank you, Marion. Here, you can take this platter to the table."

Rosemary still didn't understand why the threesome was there. Throughout lunch she kept waiting for Jason to explain it, but he seemed to be concentrating on his meal.

"How are all the men?" he finally asked.

"Good. They're good," Wes assured him.

"I paid the medical bills for you and Jesse."

"Yeah, they sent us copies. We appreciate that, Jason."

"It was the least I could do. I called the man who recommended Ted so highly and told him what he'd done. I suggested he be more circumspect about his recommendations in the future."

"Good. Ted needs to find another line of work," Wes said with satisfaction.

Rosemary remained silent. She assumed Wes had mailed her letter this morning. Jason would get it when he returned to Denver. She supposed she should tell him now, in person, but she wasn't prepared to do so in front of everyone.

At least she'd regained her composure before she saw Jason again. She wouldn't want him to know how much he'd hurt her—or know how much she loved him. That she wasn't experienced in relationships or savvy in man-woman games was something she'd take to her grave. Not that she was embarrassed about who she was. The fact that she sat here in well-worn jeans and an old sweater didn't make her any less a woman than the attractive Ms. Lock.

Just not the woman for Jason.

She listened as he and Wes continued to talk about the ranch and the cowboys who worked there. Doug, Jason's friend, asked some questions about the economics of cattle ranching. Wes filled him in hesitantly, shooting looks at Jason.

"I think I should explain that Doug is my accountant, and Marion, his wife, is my attorney," Jason said.

Rosemary looked at Jason. "I'm not opposing the sale of the ranch."

"You're not?" he asked. "But I thought we brought in enough cattle to satisfy my down payment."

"We did." She averted her eyes. It hurt too much to look at him. "But a ranch can be very demanding, especially in winter, as I'm sure your accountant realizes. I don't have the money to carry the ranch until spring. Rather than put such a strain on Sara Beth and Wes, or the men, I think I should sell the ranch." She carefully kept her gaze fixed on the table.

There was a long silence, but she didn't bother to break it.

Finally, Jason said, "Okay, if that's what you want."

She said nothing.

"I actually brought Doug and Marion along in case you wanted to make other arrangements."

"What arrangements?" Wes asked.

Rosemary said nothing.

"I thought Rosie might need a loan to get through the winter. I'm prepared to offer her operating money until fall when she can sell the yearlings."

"That's a year away!" Rosemary exclaimed, her eyes locking with his.

"Yeah, I know, but I believe you're good for it."

"And if I'm not? Where do you think I'd find the money to pay you back?"

"Or maybe I could become a silent partner in the ranch. That would leave you in charge, but I could come visit every once in a while."

Could she face him visiting, bringing beautiful women to see his investment? She didn't know if she could.

"I don't think that would work." She got up from the table. "If you'll excuse me…" She left the room before anyone could say anything.

Jason stood, but Wes put a hand on his. "I told you to clear up the business, not extend it," he muttered. "Sit down, boy. You don't want to talk to her now. Give her time to think about your offer."

Both Jason and Sara Beth protested.

"Just give her some time," Wes advised.

Jason slowly sat back down. "She didn't eat enough to keep a bird alive. Hasn't her appetite grown at all, Sara Beth?"

"She eats most days, just not as much as she used to. She's lost some weight."

"She says she's not strong enough to be a rancher," Wes said slowly. "We all want her here, but I don't know what she wants."

"Perhaps I should go talk to her," Marion said. "Do you mind, Sara Beth?"

Sara Beth nodded, then added, "Her room is the first on the left at the top of the stairs."

"Thank you." Then Marion left the kitchen to go up the stairs.

"We appreciate you trying to work out a way to keep Rosie here at the ranch," Wes told Jason. "We're all worried about her. She's not the same as she used to be since her daddy's death."

"She's had a lot to bear in the last month or so," Sara Beth said, sympathy in her voice.

"Yeah," Jason agreed, but his mind was in the room at the top of the stairs, where Marion was talking with Rosie.

Rosemary heard a soft knock on her door, but she didn't respond. She assumed whoever it was would go away.

Then she heard her door open. That could only be Sara Beth. Over her shoulder, she said, "I'm fine, Sara Beth. I just don't have much appetite today."

"I'm not Sara Beth," a low, musical voice said.

Rosemary sat up on her bed, hastily wiping the tears away. "I'm sorry, I didn't—"

"I know. And I'm being very intrusive, so I'll ask your forgiveness. But everyone downstairs is concerned about you—and what you want to do. Jason wants to find a way for you to keep the ranch. Is that not what you want?"

Rosemary sighed. "In a perfect world, that's what I would want, but I'm not strong enough to handle the ranch. That would put all the weight on Wes and Sara Beth. It's not fair to ask them to handle all the responsibility."

"They seem willing to do it. It's obvious they love you very much."

"Yes, and I love them. That's why I have to go. With Jason as the owner, they know they'll be paid promptly. They won't have to worry about some of the men being let go because I can't afford to pay them. We have a good staff of men. They deserve a good owner."

"Would you be willing to stay here and help Wes run the ranch? Jason said you're quite the cowgirl. He thinks you know what you're doing."

"He won't need me if he has Wes."

Marion paused. Then she said, "I think the

ranch needs you. All the men are worried about you. Even Jason seems to be worrying about you."

"There's no need. I can get my old job back. I called them yesterday. I'll be fine. And everyone on the ranch will be fine. The men all followed Jason's orders on the roundup, They respect him. Everyone will be okay."

"Why don't you think it over for a day or two? We'll be around. Jason promised to show us the ranch, if you don't mind."

"No, of course not."

"And you'll help Jason show us the ranch?"

"Wes can—"

"He said he'd be busy with some paperwork. Won't you help Jason?"

"Fine. If he needs me," she said, frowning.

"Great. I think Sara Beth is going to serve some delicious chocolate cake. Won't you come eat a piece?"

After a moment's hesitation, Rosemary sighed. "All right. I'll come down in a minute. I need to wash my face."

She wouldn't let Jason see her cry.

When he saw her enter the kitchen, Jason had to force himself not to jump up and embrace

Rosie. He'd missed her so much, and was afraid his offer had offended her for some reason. Why couldn't she accept the help he was offering?

Rosie was not only beautiful, but stubborn. He'd just have to keep trying.

He couldn't keep his eyes off her as they ate Sara Beth's delicious chocolate cake. If this didn't tempt Rosie's appetite, he thought, nothing would.

"I understand you and your friends are going to stay a day or two," she finally said to him.

He smiled at her. "If that's okay with you. We could stay in the nearest motel if you—"

Sara Beth stepped in. "You'll do no such thing. You'll stay right here. I'll fix the rooms right after we're finished."

"I'll help you, Sara Beth," Rosemary said.

"Lawyers can make up beds, too, Sara Beth," Marion said with a smile. "Even accountants can do it in an emergency. Right, Doug?"

"Yeah, but it's not my best talent," Doug assured his wife.

"Rosie," Jason began, "you haven't said whether you mind us staying."

She shrugged. "It doesn't much matter to me, since you're going to be the new owner."

"I thought you were going to consider my offers before making a definite decision."

"Yes, I suppose I will." But her averted gaze spoke volumes to Jason. Evidently he needed to do some major convincing.

Since they were staying, Marion asked if Jason could teach them to ride.

"I suppose, but you'd need some jeans, cowboy boots and a hat," he replied.

"Just to learn to ride?" Marion asked.

"Don't you think so, Rosie?" Jason asked, hoping to draw her into the conversation.

"It's kind of cold right now. You could wait until spring to try riding lessons."

"But that's tax time for Doug. It would be better now. Is there a store near here where we could buy those things?"

"Well, yes, but it would be expensive for just a few rides. I mean, you're not going to be here long enough to ride that much."

"But we can keep them here for when we come back, couldn't we, Jason?"

"You should be asking Rosemary that question. It's her place."

Rosemary opened her mouth to protest, but

then she closed it again. Finally she said, "Yes, of course."

"Great!" Marion exclaimed. "So can we go shopping after lunch? You'll show me what to buy, won't you, Rosemary?"

It seemed to Rosemary that everyone in the room was waiting for her answer. She nodded. "We can go to the feed store in Blue Ridge."

"Great," Marion said. "Since Doug has to go, too, why don't we all go, and then we can treat everyone to dinner, to thank you for your hospitality. You won't have to do the dishes tonight, Sara Beth!"

Sara Beth grinned. "Young lady, I like the way you think. Don't you, Rosie?"

In spite of herself, Rosemary had to agree. She liked Marion. Especially since she was married.

Blue Ridge was a small town, but for the people in the area, it had everything they'd ever need. Still, Rosemary couldn't help worry what Marion would think of it.

"Are we really going to a feed store?" the lawyer asked in surprise as Jason pulled up in front of it.

"They sell everything here," Rosemary said.

And almost two hours later it seemed as if Marion had bought everything. With Lou, the proprietor, smiling and waving goodbye, they left the store, each of them laden down with packages.

"That was fun," Marion said as they put the packages in the truck. "Now where do we go eat?"

"There's really only one restaurant," Rosemary said. "The café across the street."

She expected Marion to scoff at the lack of choice but she couldn't have been more wrong.

"Well, it may not have cooking as good as Sara Beth's but we've got to give her a break."

Before Rosemary realized what he was doing, Jason had put his arm around her as they walked across the street.

"Jason! What are you doing?"

"I'm escorting the only eligible woman across the street. I can tell you Doug would be upset if I escorted Marion, and Wes has already warned me about sweet-talking Sara Beth."

She gave him a sharp look, but what he said made sense...she guessed. So for a few minutes, she could experience Jason "taking care" of her, as he had on the cattle drive.

When they got to the café, Sara Beth told them what she thought they made well, and they all took her advice. There was a lot of conversation around the table, and Rosemary found herself drawn into it, much to her surprise. Marion was entertaining and drew everyone in with her enthusiasm.

"I can't wait until morning when I can dress up like a cowboy and get on a horse. I've never done that before. Does it hurt?"

"Um, maybe a little bit. Just take it slowly at first," Rosemary suggested.

"Yeah, don't start with a day-long ride like I did," Jason advised.

"But you'd ridden before, hadn't you?" Marion asked.

"Yeah, but I wasn't used to that much riding. Rosie, of course, rode like a pro, not showing any discomfort."

"Really? Can you teach me how to ride, Rosemary? Jason can teach Doug. He can be grumpy if he's uncomfortable."

"Then we'll definitely leave him to Jason," Rosemary said, smiling at Marion, as if she were her friend. She was enjoying female companionship of her own age.

"So I get stuck with Grumpy here? That

doesn't seem fair," Jason protested, but they all realized he was teasing.

"Maybe Rosemary will allow us to work together so you won't be alone with Doug," Marion suggested.

"How about it, Rosie? Will you team up with me, so I won't be stuck with Doug?"

The last thing she wanted to do was spend more time with Jason, but she'd been raised to extend courtesy to guests.

"I—I suppose we could join forces."

"Terrific. I can't wait until tomorrow." Jason shot her a dazzling smile that took her off guard and tingled all the way to her toes.

And suddenly she realized that in spite of all the warnings she'd issued to herself, she wanted nothing more than to spend time with Jason. No matter how dangerous it was. No matter how short.

After this, she'd probably never see him again.

CHAPTER TWELVE

THE first person she saw enter the kitchen was Jason. He came through the doorway with a cheery good-morning greeting, surprising Rosie while she was flipping the last of the flapjacks she was making for breakfast, along with Sara Beth.

He never looked more handsome. His skin glistened from a shower and shave, and he smelled fresh, like the outdoors she loved so much. His hair was still slightly damp, darkening the milk-chocolate color to a bittersweet chocolate.

And bittersweet it was.

Rosie knew this was probably the last day she'd spend with Jason. After she'd told him her final decision, he and his lawyer and accountant would no doubt be holed up tomorrow with final preparations for the closing. She'd tell Wes to handle it, basically to give Jason everything he wanted.

And then she'd be packing up to leave. She'd made arrangements to stay with a friend back in Cheyenne till she found an apartment. At least she'd been able to get her job back. The publicity work was enjoyable and fun, but, she had to admit, nowhere near as fulfilling as ranching. It was in her blood.

But she had to say goodbye to the Bar G. She had no choice.

First she had to teach Marion and Doug to ride. It would be one of the last things she'd do on the ranch.

As if on cue, the couple strode into the kitchen then, dressed in their new cowboy clothes and smiles, till they saw breakfast on the table already.

"I'm sorry I overslept," Marion said. "I should have been down here to help out. Is there something I can do?"

"Nonsense," Sara Beth assured her. "You're our guests. Just sit down and eat." She gave the city slickers a sly grin. "You'll need every ounce of energy when these two get you on a horse." She nodded at Rosie and Jason.

Marion gave off a nervous laugh as she exchanged a skeptical look with her husband. "That doesn't sound encouraging."

Jason sidled up close to Rosemary and mock-whispered, "Sara Beth is going to ruin our plan of torturing them."

His warm breath stirred the few strands of hair that never stayed in her braid, and sent gooseflesh up and down her arms. Surreptitiously she stepped aside and forced a laugh. "Just ignore Jason," she told the Locks. "It's going to be fun." And she was honestly looking forward to the day. Despite her looming departure, she was enjoying Marion's and Doug's company. And Jason's.

Last night after they'd come back from dinner, the two women had taken on the men in a game of cards and two hours of laughter later, they'd emerged victorious. It had been the only time she'd laughed since…well, since before her father had died and she'd returned to the Bar G. It had felt good.

That was what life was supposed to feel like, she reminded herself. A person was supposed to laugh, to be in the company of friends and the people she loved. Well, at least she'd have half of that when she returned to Cheyenne. She'd have her city friends, her work friends, though she'd be leaving behind her best friends, Wes and Sara Beth. And the man she loved.

She shook herself out of the reverie before depression overcame her. Pasting on a smile, she said to Marion and Doug, "Don't you worry about riding. Just remember, you can stop whenever you want."

Marion put an arm around her. "I like you better than Jason." She took the platter of flap-jacks from Rosie after she placed the last one on the stack, and carried it to the table. "Let's eat. I need my strength," she joked.

After breakfast, when Wes went into the office to do paperwork, and Sara Beth cleaned the kitchen, the foursome bundled up and headed to the barn. The day was sunny but had a chill in the air.

Rosemary introduced the Locks to the horses they'd be riding. Then she left the basic instruction for Jason to impart. She had to admit the man knew his horses. He looked equally comfortable here in the barn as he did in his high-rise Denver office. And just as adept. She knew her assessment of him was on target. He would make a great ranch owner, and though she'd be sad to leave, she looked forward to the improvements he'd make on the Bar G. Just for that reason she felt her parents would approve of her decision. Their land would flourish.

When Marion was ready to mount up, Rosie had her get to know her horse first. "Her name is Daisy. She's very gentle and patient." She showed her how to rub the mare's nose and pat her, and in no time Marion made friends with the horse. Until she tried to mount.

She started and stopped a few times, awkwardly lifting her leg and losing her grip on the pommel. Rosie quickly moved to assist her, and with great effort Marion finally sat the horse.

"Please tell me this is the hardest part," she said, letting out a deep sigh.

Rosemary just smiled.

She handed the woman Daisy's reins and led her out to the corral. "Just relax in the saddle and move with the horse. You're going to start off real slow. Just walking around the corral."

Looking downright terrified, Marion squeaked out, "That sounds good to me."

Despite her fear, Marion caught on quickly and with each turn around the corral she got more comfortable.

Just as Rosie got less comfortable.

Right in front of her Jason led Doug around on his horse. Seeing him in the saddle made her remember the days and nights of the roundup. How they'd ridden side by side herding in the errant cows. How he'd looked after her after Wes had ridden in. How he'd kissed her …

But those kisses hadn't meant anything, she reminded herself sternly. She couldn't lose sight of the truth, no matter how much she yearned for Jason to take her in his arms and kiss her for real.

"You've got it bad for him, don't you?"

She was so caught up in her thoughts, she barely heard Marion's question. "I—I don't know what you mean," she stammered to buy herself some time.

"Jason." She nodded ahead. "You're in love with him, aren't you?"

Rosie faked a laugh. "That's ridiculous! I could never love a man like him."

Marion smiled. "Funny, that's just what he said."

Her curiosity piqued, in spite of herself, Rosie asked, "What do you mean?"

"Jason told us all about you, and every time he said you could never love a man like him.

Someone who'd taken away your family heritage."

Rosie barely heard everything Marion said. She'd been caught up in her first words. Jason told them all about her? She asked, "He—he talked about me?"

"All the time. For weeks now you're all he's talked about. I think that's why I get along so well with you. I felt like I knew you before I even met you."

"But I would think he'd had enough of me on the roundup. I was quite a responsibility for him."

Marion shook her head and then gripped the reins tighter when she slid a bit in the saddle. "That's not how he described you, Rosie. Every time he said your name I swear I could hear birds singing and bells ringing," she said on a high-pitched laugh.

Rosie felt her cheeks redden and immediately put her head down. "I—I'm sure you're exaggerating." If Jason had had any interest in her at all, he'd have shown it, not walk away without saying goodbye and let weeks pass without contacting her. No, he only had interest in the ranch.

The ranch that would soon be his. She'd just be a memory.

Marion let out an exasperated sigh that had
nothing to do with her horse or her no-doubt
sore bottom. "Sometimes I don't understand
people! Do I have to lead them around
like…like a horse?" Not giving Rosie a chance
to ask what she was talking about, Marion
called out to Jason in front of them.

He turned and the sunlight lit his jaw, all that
was visible under the brim of his tan cowboy
hat. "What is it?"

Marion stopped her horse and took on the
voice she probably used in the courtroom.
"Jason Barton, why have you not told
Rosemary how you feel about her?"

Jason's head jerked up, and his face
blanched. "What?"

"I said, why have you not told Rosemary
how you feel about her." Marion seemed to be
quickly losing her patience with her friend.

"I…" Jason stopped, then tried again. But
he still wouldn't look at Rosie. "I didn't think
I should until after she made her decision
about the ranch."

Rosie felt her heart pick up, her blood pound
in her ears. Had she heard him right? "What
are you trying to say, Jason?"

He looked at her then and his eyes were as

blue as the sky. "I wanted to tell you, Rosie, but Wes kept telling me to wait until the ranch was settled. I was afraid you wouldn't believe me if I was still trying to buy the Bar G."

Her chest was so tight, she could barely draw the breath to say, "Believe you about what?"

"That I love you."

"You love me?" She couldn't believe her own ears.

"Didn't you guess, Rosie? I tried to tell you, but—well, things got in the way. The ranch got in the way."

"But I can't keep the ranch. How would I know if you loved me or the ranch?" Her hands were shaking so much, she stuck them in her jeans pockets.

Jason alit from his horse and strode toward her. Looking up at her, he asked, "You mean if I buy the ranch, then you'll know I love you?"

"I know that doesn't sound right. But I thought if you were trying to get the ranch, you might not really care about me." More than anything she wanted to reach out to him, to feel him against her, but she couldn't trust her legs to get off Maggie. She was shaking so much, she feared they wouldn't support her.

"Damn it, Rosie, I'm in love with you. I've been in love with you since the first time I saw you in your jeans and boots. The more time I spent with you, the more I knew you were the one I wanted." He bowed his head in a sheepish gesture. "I've been trying to figure out a way for you to keep the ranch so I'd know you love me and not my money."

"Jason, I love you, too," she confessed. "I fell in love with you when you were trying to handle the roundup for me. You worked so hard when it wasn't to your benefit. And you kissed me—"

It was as if the mere mention of the word put him in mind of kissing Rosie. In one swift, sure motion he reached out and lifted her off the saddle, took her in his arms and kissed her.

His kiss stole her breath, buckled her knees and she fell into his arms. He used his lips to tell her how much he loved her, and she did the same. She made a small moan when he pulled his mouth away.

He smiled slyly. "I thought you hated it when I kissed you."

"Just when I thought you were pretending to like me to convince the cowboys we were together." Her pulse was still racing so fast, she thought she'd pass out.

"I guess I forgot to tell you I wasn't pretending."

"I wish you had."

"Me, too. You kiss a lot better when you mean it." And he took her mouth again, to prove it.

"Why didn't you call me, Jason?" she asked when she could.

"Wes kept telling me to wait until he talked to you."

Her brows knit together. "He never talked to me about you. He tried to convince me to keep the ranch and try to make a go of it."

"He didn't want you to go. No one did. I didn't want you to go, either." He lifted her chin up with a curled index finger and looked deeply into her eyes. "I want you to stay and take me on, too. Will you, Rosie?"

"Oh, Jason, I love you so much." She kissed him then, and he wrapped his arms around her even tighter, as if to keep her from leaving. Not that she'd make any effort to do so.

"I think we're going to be on these horses for a while, eh, Doug?" she heard Marion say.

Breaking away from Jason, Rosie looked

over her shoulder at the woman. She and Jason had been so caught up in each other, they'd forgotten their riders.

Marion looked at them with feigned impatience. "I'm not getting down without some help."

She helped Marion down, as Jason did the same for Doug.

"Thanks, Rosie," she said with a smile.

"Thank you," Rosie replied. "If you hadn't forced Jason's hand…"

"We women have to stick together."

Jason reached out then and grabbed Rosie's hand, pulling her toward him. "*This* woman's sticking to no one but me." He took her in his arms, and glanced over at his friends. "Can't a guy get some privacy?"

Smiling broadly, Marion and Doug linked hands and started out of the corral.

"You should take a good long soak in the tub," Rosie called after them. She knew their muscles would be screaming real soon.

Marion looked over her shoulder and teased, "And what are you two going to be doing while we soak?"

Jason laughed. "We'll think of something." And he pulled Rosie toward the barn.

When they'd cleared the door they went into each other's arms. "We've got a lot of talking to do, Rosie. A lot of planning. But first—"

The barn door opened and Sara Beth came in, a stainless steel bucket in her hand. She started when she saw them in an embrace in a darkened corner of the barn. "What's going on with you two?"

Jason grinned. "We're in love, Sara Beth! Isn't it great?"

Sara Beth's face lit up in a big smile. "It's wonderful! Wait until I tell Wes!"

But Jason stopped her. "Wait. I want some time alone with Rosie before you tell him. He's been keeping us apart."

"He has?"

"Yeah. Every time I called, he kept telling me to wait. That's why I'm here. I got tired of waiting."

Sara Beth shook her head. "I've got to do some things in here. You two go into the family room. You'll be alone there."

Rosie and Jason did as she suggested. Before she could sit on the oversize sofa, he took her in his arms. "Rosie, you do believe me, don't you?"

"About what?"

"That I'm not marrying you to get the ranch."

"I believe you. You've tried too hard to give it to me. I know you really love me." Her eyes filled with tears of happiness.

His lips covered hers, and Rosie knew she'd never get tired of kissing this man. No one else had ever aroused her as much with one kiss, never convinced her of his deep affection, as Jason. He moved into a big chair and sat down, pulling Rosie into his lap.

She lay her head on his shoulder. "Jason this is so hard to believe."

He unzipped her coat and then his. "I'm working hard at convincing you, sweetheart. This is what I wanted to do every night on the roundup. But that wasn't possible, with all the cowboys ready to jump to your defense if I made a move to hold you like this."

"Well, they're kind of like my big brothers."

"Yeah, but will they accept me as your husband?"

Rosemary stared at him solemnly. "I think so if you buy the ranch and then marry me. They'll know you really love me that way."

"Done!" He kissed her again. "I could do this all day long."

"You wouldn't get any complaints from me," she said, a dreamy smile on her face.

"So, when can we get married?"

"I don't even know that much about you!"

"What do you want to know? You know I've been married before. She was interested in my money more than me. And she expected everything to be given to her. That's what impressed me most about you. You were willing to work so hard for the ranch. You could've stayed home and sent Wes on the roundup, but you didn't."

She played with a button on his shirt. "That's what attracted you to me?"

"No, honey. But that's why I first got interested in you. When you came to my office, I noticed, uh, your charms. But my wife was beautiful, too. So I was determined to ignore any attraction I felt. But when you appeared in your jeans and boots, ready to get on a horse and chase after cows, I was a goner."

"Really?" Rosemary said, looking at him from under her lashes.

"Don't play coy with me, young lady! When did you fall for me?"

"I was attracted to you when I saw you, too, but you were a millionaire. I needed your agreement to keep my ranch, but I didn't expect you to work so hard for me to win. When you tried to care for me when I was sick, not letting me give up, fighting for me to keep the ranch, I knew I loved you, too, but I didn't think you cared about me. I've been so depressed since I realized I couldn't keep the ranch or you. I thought I had to let the two most important things in my life go away."

"If I had to move back to Denver, would you go with me?" he asked.

"Yes," she said at once, "but I'd rather stay here."

With a grin, he said, "Me, too."

She hit him with her fist. "Were you testing me?"

"Yeah. But I had to ask. Now let's start making plans."

"For what?" she asked, a little confused.

"We love each other. The next step is to marry. You will marry me, won't you, sweetheart?"

Her answer took several seconds and didn't involve any conversation until she finally said, "Of course I will."

"I'll give you a little time if you need it. I know I'm rushing you," Jason said.

"I don't need time," she replied. "I always wanted to be swept off my feet!"

"Good. Then let's get married at once, unless you want a fairy-tale wedding?"

"No. But I would like to go to Denver and do some shopping. Maybe Marion would return the favor and help me shop in her territory."

"I think she might. She and Doug have been trying to get me married for a while now. They were worried about me being alone."

"Well, you're mine now, so don't you forget it!"

"No chance. How long do you need to shop?"

"Probably a week."

"Okay, I'll stay here on the ranch and see what I think needs to be done. You go to Denver with Doug and Marion. You can stay in my condo. But only a week. Then you come home and we get our license and get married. Because if you take longer than a week, I'll come after you."

"Jason? Rosie? Wes wants to know what you're doing all alone in there," Sara Beth said from the door without opening it.

"It's okay, Sara Beth," Jason called. "You can open the door."

Sara Beth did so but didn't come in. "Wes is worrying about you two. Can you come reassure him?"

"Yeah, we'll be right there."

When they entered the kitchen, Wes was sitting at the table, with a frown on his face.

Jason spoke first. "Wes, Rosie and I would like to get married. We're hoping you'll give us your blessing."

Wes stared at him. Then his gaze moved to Rosie. "You sure about this, Rosie?"

"Oh, yes. I'm very sure."

"So you'll get married next year?"

Jason shook his head. "More like a week."

"Good. I don't want you two spending too much time alone before the wedding. I promised her daddy."

Rosie hid a blush. "I don't think you promised that to Dad!"

"I promised him I'd take care of you."

"Good. Then you can give me away, just as if you were my dad. Is that okay?"

"I guess so," Wes agreed, but Rosie saw the pride in his eyes.

"And you and Sara Beth will be grandparents for our children," Jason said. "And we plan to have a lot of them."

"Oh, really?" Rosemary asked, since they hadn't discussed that subject.

Jason hurriedly corrected himself. "If my wife agrees."

With a smile, Rosemary said, "She agrees. And we're going to pass our ranch to the next generation, just like Mom did.

* * * * *

Gwen took a taxi to the Yellow Parrot, and with each passing block she grew more tense. It didn't take a rocket scientist to figure out that this dive was in the worst part of town. Gwen had learned to take care of herself, but the minute she entered the bar, she realized that a smart woman would have brought a gun with her. The interior was hot, smelly and dirty, and the air was so smoky that it looked as if a pea soup fog had settled inside the building. Before she had gone three feet, an old drunk came up to her and asked for money. Sidestepping him, she searched for someone who looked as if he or she might actually work here, someone other than the prostitutes who were trolling for customers.

After fending off a couple of grasping young men and ignoring several vulgar propositions in an odd mixture of Spanish and

English, Gwen found the bar. She ordered a beer from the burly, bearded bartender. When he set the beer in front of her, she took the opportunity to speak to him.

"I'm looking for a man. An older American man, in his seventies. He was probably with a younger woman. This man is my father and—"

"*No hablo inglés.*"

"Oh." He didn't speak English and she didn't speak Spanish. Now what?

While she was considering her options, Gwen noticed a young man in skintight black pants and an open black shirt, easing closer and closer to her as he made his way past the other men at the bar.

Great. That was all she needed—some horny young guy mistaking her for a prostitute.

"*Señorita.*" His voice was softly accented and slightly slurred. His breath smelled of liquor. "You are all alone, *sí?*"

"Please, go away," Gwen said. "I'm not interested."

He laughed, as if he found her attitude amusing. "Then it is for me to make you interested. I am Marco. And you are…?"

"Leaving," Gwen said.

She realized it had been a mistake to come

here alone tonight. Any effort to unearth information about her father in a place like this was probably pointless. She would do better to come back tomorrow and try to speak to the owner. But when she tried to move past her ardent young suitor, he reached out and grabbed her arm. She tensed.

Looking him right in the eyes, she told him, "Let go of me. Right now."

"But you cannot leave. The night is young."

Gwen tugged on her arm, trying to break free. He tightened his hold, his fingers biting into her flesh. With her heart beating rapidly as her basic fight-or-flight instinct kicked in, she glared at the man.

"I'm going to ask you one more time to let me go."

Grinning smugly, he grabbed her other arm, holding her in place.

Suddenly, seemingly from out of nowhere, a big hand clamped down on Marco's shoulder, jerked him back and spun him around. Suddenly free, Gwen swayed slightly but managed to retain her balance as she watched in amazement as a tall, lanky man in jeans and cowboy boots shoved her would-be suitor up against the bar.

"I believe the lady asked you real nice to let her go," the man said, in a deep Texas drawl. "Where I come from, a gentleman respects a lady's wishes."

Marco grumbled something unintelligible in Spanish. Probably cursing, Gwen thought. Or maybe praying. If she were Marco, she would be praying that the big, rugged American wouldn't beat her to a pulp.

Apparently Marco was not as smart as she was. When the Texan released him, he came at her rescuer, obviously intending to fight him. The Texan took Marco out with two swift punches, sending the younger man to the floor. Gwen glanced down at where Marco lay sprawled flat on his back, unconscious.

Her hero turned to her. "Ma'am, are you all right?"

She nodded. The man was about six-two, with a sunburned tan, sun-streaked brown hair and azure-blue eyes.

"What's a lady like you doing in a place like this?" he asked.

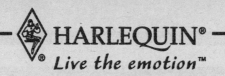

HARLEQUIN®
INTRIGUE®

BREATHTAKING ROMANTIC SUSPENSE

Shared dangers and passions lead to electrifying
romance and heart-stopping suspense!

Every month, you'll meet six new heroes
who are guaranteed to make your spine tingle
and your pulse pound. With them you'll enter
into the exciting world of Harlequin Intrigue—
where your life is on the line
and so is your heart!

THAT'S INTRIGUE—
ROMANTIC SUSPENSE
AT ITS BEST!

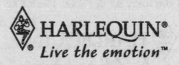

HARLEQUIN®
Presents

The world's bestselling romance series...
The series that brings you your favorite authors,
month after month:

Helen Bianchin...Emma Darcy
Lynne Graham...Penny Jordan
Miranda Lee...Sandra Marton
Anne Mather...Carole Mortimer
Susan Napier...Michelle Reid

and many more uniquely talented authors!

Wealthy, powerful, gorgeous men...
Women who have feelings just like your own...
The stories you love, set in exotic, glamorous locations...

HARLEQUIN®
Presents

Seduction and Passion Guaranteed!

www.eHarlequin.com

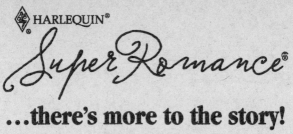
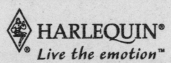